Get Me Out Of Here –

I'm A Headteacher

Dedicated to my wife, Alison and my daughters, Erin and

Rachel, and all the people who acted like nothing was wrong!

Introduction

It was the start of the second term at Hilltop Primary, as the 1990s drifted gently by. My first term as the new head teacher had been hectic and chaotic and I was now eighteen years older than I had been in September. But I had settled in well and become used to the idiosyncrasies of my staff; Ann, the secretary, who was flummoxed by anything more technologically complex than a biro; Walt, the caretaker, whose love of his urinals transcended most people's love of life itself; and Alan Barnett, the Y6 teacher who could not only make a mountain out of a molehill, but could also get stuck half way up said mountain, breaking his beard on a perilous precipice before crashing back to the ground, injuring several bystanders on the way.

Over the course of the first term I had appointed a belching cleaner, averted a crisis concerning a group of knife-wielding new-age travellers and been tempted to give out detentions to parents who had taken to fighting on the school yard. So far I had not written my resignation letter, but only, perhaps, because I hadn't had the time!

But now, all the woes of the first term were over and the New Year signalled a new start. The building of the new classroom was well under way, if by well under way we were to mean stalling at every turn and becoming an object of ridicule. Now that Christmas was over it seemed safe to assume that things should progress smoothly for the school as we headed into spring. However, that assumption failed to take into account a full blown Ofsted inspection, the most disastrous fire drill in the entire history of disastrous fire drills and all-out war between Walt and the Lord Mayor.

Spring Term: Week 1

My dad left us on Christmas Eve...

The weather over the Christmas holiday had been cruel. It had been intensely cold and had snowed on many occasions. The snow had frozen and then with more snow falling on top the roads were now treacherous. Early on this January morning the school drive, with its gentle slope, had become a white-knuckle ride. The curve at the bottom of the drive was probably the most fearsome thing I had seen since catching sight of Gillian in her jungle dress. And as I inched my car toward the car park my thoughts were no longer on either the pleasures of the holiday or the worries of the new term. My thoughts were on keeping my car the same shape as when I left home this morning.

It was with a sense of relief that I parked and climbed out of my car, only to hear the stomach-churning crunch of metal on metal. Amanda Chaplin had slid down the drive and glided gracefully into the metal fence that separated cars from pedestrians. Understandably upset, she climbed out of her car and slipped on the ice, landing flat on her back. I rushed down to help her, barely able to stand on the layers of compacted ice. Within seconds I caught sight of Gillian's car turning into the drive and I frantically waved to her as a signal to stay where she was. Never one to take advice, Gillian came down the drive at her usual speed and upon seeing the predicament ahead of her, braked and slid like an overweight metal swan into the rear of Amanda's car.

Walt had been busy throwing grit on the playground in an attempt to avoid too many broken legs but, on hearing the increasing number of crunching noises, he decided to come and investigate. As always, he was quick to assess the situation. "You've hit that fence!" he told Amanda. "And then it looks like you've slid straight into her, nah then!" he advised Gillian. He was mind-blowingly accurate on both counts. "I'll tell you this and I'll tell you now, it's a bugger is that drive when it's got some ice on it." he continued. Amanda and Gillian nodded, agreeing that the drive was indeed a bugger when it was covered in ice, but both were rather more concerned about their immediate situation.

As Gillian moved her car carefully away from the scene, Walt took a moment to draw deep breaths as he inspected the damage around the front of Amanda's car. "It's going to need a complete new section, this is. It's beyond repair. I wouldn't have thought it could make such a mess, nah then!"

Amanda, looking very concerned at this point, asked Walt to explain a little more. "How do you mean, a new section? Will they have to replace the entire front of my car? I hope they don't decide to write it off, I really don't need the hassle."

"They won't write your car off, you bloody pancake. It only needs a new bumper and a bit of paintwork!" Walt somewhat paradoxically replied.

"But I thought you said it's beyond repair." Amanda protested.

"I'm talking about my bloody fence! You've buggered my entire panel. That'll have to come out and be replaced. Your car's alright. There's nowt wrong wi' your car save for a bit of cosmopolitan damage."

Today's sunshine concerned me because there was a chance that it would lead to legal proceedings. To explain, the school yard was iced over and if a child fell and broke a bone, the school could be accused of not taking due care of its pupils. To counter this, Walt had thrown grit and salt on the yard in order to melt the ice. Thus, if a child now fell and suffered not only a wound, but one infected by grit, the school could once again be accused of not taking due care of its pupils. The fact that Walt had used grit would show that the yard was felt to be unsafe and this would not go in our favour. And if Walt had 'missed a bit' then all hell could break loose if a child fell on that particular part of the yard. Of course, if the yard had not been gritted at all, that would show that we didn't take due care of our pupils. If it could only rain, the children could be legitimately kept indoors and the problem would cease to exist. Unfortunately, it was not going to rain today so I steeled myself for the first fallen angel, followed by the customary solicitor's letter.

But it was the events at the end of the day that took my attention most of all. A phone call from a lady called Mrs. Edlington was the cause of my concern. Mrs. Edlington had a son aged eight. He was called Edward and was always a pleasant child whenever I had come across him. So it was something of a surprise when Edward's mother launched a vicious diatribe at me over the telephone. Her claim was, not that he had fallen on the yard and suffered an injured shoe lace, but that he was being bullied. He had, according to the expressive and articulate Mrs. Edlington, been set upon by a bunch of bleeding thugs what were older than our Edward. They had repeatedly punched him and kicked him. They had kicked footballs at him and made threats regarding what they might do to him on his journey to or from school. As a result, he was terrified to come to school tomorrow. It appeared that, despite all these attacks taking place, the little bastards had not been reprimanded, she explained. The teachers apparently, did nothing.

This conversation puzzled me, as bullying was always something I came down heavily on. I found it hard to reconcile the fact that nobody did anything to sort out the problem. I also found it strange that none of this had come to my attention during the day. After all, it all sounded pretty serious. I promised Mrs. Edlington that I would talk to the staff who had been supervising the yard, right away. I would then deal with the bullies first thing in the morning. I also impressed upon her that Edward must come to school, otherwise the bullies would have won.

Celia and Alma had been supervising the yard today, so I went to see them immediately. Each of them told me that nobody had reported anyone being hurt and that they had not seen anything even remotely reminiscent of a bullying incident. This was odd.

Other children adore getting their friends into trouble and if these attacks had taken place as Edward had described, I would have expected the children to be reporting the situation in their droves. It's what primary school children do well, to use one of Alan's phrases.

The following morning I apprehended Edward and took him to my office. I asked him to describe who had attacked him and what they did. He gave me the names of three boys in the oldest class and described a rather brutal attack which apparently took place on the playground whilst Celia and Alma were supervising. I now had two jobs to do. The first was to quickly warn today's playground supervisors to keep a close eye on the situation. The second was to round up the three attackers and find out what was happening.

The three boys looked at me with glazed expressions as I asked them to explain what they did to Edward. One of the boys claimed he had no idea who Edward was and the other two knew of him but had been playing football at the other end of the yard during every break time yesterday. Being a teacher is a little like being a detective sometimes – you get a strong feeling about whether someone is being truthful or winding you up. The trouble was, I genuinely believed these boys were telling the truth. This and the fact that Edward had no obvious marks on his body from any attack made me wonder what exactly was going on.

I had no reports of bullying from the supervising staff throughout the day. Edward never appeared at my door to complain of an incident so I assumed that things must have been fine. But at three-fifty, a phone call from Edward's mother changed all that. He had been bullied again today. And now her accusations were pernicious. She was going to attain maximum publicity about the way her son's bullying was being ignored. She was going to complain to the Education Department that we were sweeping her son's problems under the carpet. If necessary, she was going to get legal advice and sue the school for allowing her child to be mentally tortured whilst nothing was done to help him. And I believed every word she said.

I was intensely worried about the situation. If the boy was being bullied I wanted to stop it as much as his mother did. But there was nothing to suggest there was anything happening. He had no bruises or cuts, other children had neither seen nor reported anything, staff had seen nothing to concern them despite specifically keeping an eye on this boy. And yet Mrs. Edlington was convinced that she was sending her son to a school where nobody cared about his welfare and she was more than prepared to make everyone else believe this too. And I had no idea how to stop her.

I looked at the playground rota for the next day. Edward's class teacher, Paul, was on duty and I went to warn him of the situation.

"Keep an eye on Edward Edlington on the yard tomorrow, Paul. His mother claims he's being bullied but we can't find any evidence. Has he been OK in class?"

"He's been alright, yeah. Poor little devil, bullying's the last thing he needs right now!" Paul said.

"How do you mean?" I asked.

"Well, I had the kids writing things about their Christmas holidays when they came back on Monday. Most of them wrote about two pages but Edward wrote one line. I was going to give him hell and then I read it. 'My dad left us on Christmas Eve'. He didn't put anything else. Not a lot you can follow that with though, is there!"

"His dad left them on Christmas Eve? And is that true, did he?"

"Apparently. And he's not been back since, according to Edward."

"Cheers Paul. I think you've just solved it."

"How do you mean?"

"If it's what I think it is, he's… I'll tell you tomorrow after I've checked out my theory."

At the first break time I went into a classroom and looked out onto the yard. I spent the whole break there, watching Edward and what he was doing was both amazing and very, very sad. When the children came back inside I picked up the phone and called Mrs. Edlington. I invited her to come into school in time for the afternoon break. I gave her a firm arrival time and told her to come to my office and under no circumstances to let Edward see her. Reluctantly she agreed to my request.

She arrived at one-fifty and sat, stony-faced in my office. "Trying to weedle out of it are you!" She snapped. "I knew you'd get worried when I mentioned the newspapers and things. Well you won't get round me with cups of coffee and smart talk. I'm here to protect my kid."

"Mrs. Edlington, I don't want to get into an argument right now. Like you, I also want to protect your son and I've been as concerned as you have over these allegations."

"They're not allegations! He's being bullied. I'm not having no cover up."

"I promise you there's no cover up. Come with me please."

I led her down the corridor and into the classroom where I had spent the morning break. From there we had an uninterrupted view of the yard. I pointed out her son to her and asked her to watch carefully.

Edward played alone for a moment and then, uncharacteristically ran up to one of the biggest boys in the school and thumped him in the back. The boy ignored Edward, save for telling him to go away. Edward did not go away but instead returned and kicked the boy on the leg. Once again, the boy told him to go and then carried on playing a game. Over the next ten minutes Edward proceeded to taunt four children. Each of his 'victims' was in the oldest class and each was bigger and stronger than most of the children in the school. I was very proud of the fact that each boy tried to tolerate Edward rather than turning on him. By the end of the break, Mrs. Edlington was fully aware that it was Edward who was the problem here and that the other children were remaining remarkably controlled whilst he attempted to wind them up.

"The little sod!" she growled. "Just wait till I get him home. I'll beat him black and blue. Putting me to all this trouble. The little git!"

I invited her back to my office. There was something I wanted to explain to her.

"I hope this doesn't feel like too much of an intrusion, but yesterday I learned about your husband leaving home at Christmas." I began.

"That's got nowt to do wi' our Edward being bullied!" She snapped back at me.

"Let me explain. Edward's had a shock, just like you have. His dad's walked out and left him and Edward will feel a sense of responsibility for that. You see, children at Edward's age are still a little egocentric. They still tend to think that the world revolves around them – they don't fully understand that other factors might be involved. Edward's too young to be aware of all the complexities of an adult relationship. Whatever problems you and Mr. Edlington had are meaningless to Edward. Money, social lives, work, affairs or anything else that can upset adults are way out of a child's league. He is aware of one thing only – his dad was supposed to love him and instead, he's walked out and left him. To Edward this means his dad doesn't love him and if that's the case, Edward will be thinking that something he's done has stopped his dad from loving him. If you and your husband had arguments, it's likely that Edward thought they were about him in some way. And now, as far as he's concerned, his dad has left him – he's not left you in Edward's eyes – he's left Edward."

"So why is he giving me a hard time? Why is he pretending that he's being bullied and putting me to all this trouble if it's nowt to do with his dad and me falling out?"

"You've got to think of this from the point of view of a child who thinks he's just driven one of his parents away. Edward feels responsible that his dad left. He thinks he's upset his dad so much that it's stopped him loving him and wanting to be with him. And worst of all, he doesn't actually know what it was that he did wrong. What will happen next in Edward's view of the world? He's driven his dad away, isn't it only a matter of time before his mum leaves him as well? He thinks it's all down to him, Mrs. Edlington. If his dad can stop loving him, then so can his mum and he's terrified that one day he'll go home from school and you won't be there. The only way he can think of to make sure that doesn't happen is to stay home from school and be with you. But to do that he has to give you a damn good reason. He can't pretend to be ill because you probably won't get taken in by it and even if you do, he can't make it last for too long. So he's invented the bullying story. It's a sympathy vote that he believed would work. And in order to perpetuate it he needed some evidence and that's why he's taunting the older kids. He wants someone to hit him so that he's got some physical proof for his story. And if we hadn't found out so quickly, the next step would have been for him to hurt himself on purpose. He's scared, Mrs. Edlington. He's not causing you trouble to get back at you. He's making a desperate attempt to stop you from leaving him because he loves you. He needs to know that whatever happens between you and your husband, he is not to blame. He needs to know that you are both going to carry on loving him and caring for him, even if you can't always be together as a family. He needs to feel secure."

Mrs. Edlington gazed at the window. There were tears in her eyes and she swallowed heavily. She blinked hard and turned to face me, her eyes reddening and her voice shaking as she spoke. "We didn't know we were upsetting him. Kids are tough, aren't they? They adapt to things. I never thought he'd have all that going on in his head. I'd have talked to him about it. I would!"

"People always say that kids adapt to things. In reality, what choice do they have? If a parent walks out then, yes, the kids adapt, they have to. But that doesn't mean they're happy. You can't lose everything you thought was permanent and be happy about it. You have to learn that your life will be different from now on. You won't be able to do all of the things you used to do. You'll look back and wish it could all be like it was, but you know it can't. That's what adapting is for a child. And children worry about the little things that adults tend to ignore. They will trace everything back to an insignificant event and take all the blame for a family break up. And as a parent you have to reassure. You might not be able to promise a happy family any more, but you can reassure Edward that he is not the cause of the problem. Tell him you're always going to be there for him."

She nodded and rubbed her eyes.

"I'm going to work in the secretary's office." I said. "I'll bring Edward over and I want you to stay and have a chat in my office. I think you've both got a lot to talk about."

I stood in Ann's office and smiled. "So many days you run around like a headless chicken, trying to solve problems and sort out disasters. You end up knackered and despondent at the end of it all and you can't even put your finger on one thing you've achieved. But something like that makes all the difference. That woman and her son are beginning a whole new relationship in my office. For the first time in ages, they're talking to each other and actually listening to each other. That's what this job should be about some of the time. It won't show up on any progress profiles but I feel like I've made a bit of a difference. I think I'm going to go home feeling good tonight for a change."

Ann had an awkwardness about her body posture. She had wanted to interrupt but she could see I was feeling the need to ramble on and she clearly wanted to give me a little space in which to be proud. But now that I had finally shut up, she looked me in the eye and spoke unusually solemnly. "We had a late mail delivery. I think you should take a look." She handed me a brown envelope addressed simply to 'The Headteacher' with the school's full postal address under it.

I took out the letter and glanced casually at it. My school was going to be subjected to a full inspection. In just four weeks' time a team of four inspectors would descend upon us and look into every aspect of teaching, planning, financial control, health and safety, governors' meetings, strategic plans, policies, long term development plans, long term financial plans, discipline, community involvement, parental involvement, staff contracts, pupil test performance, business links and a whole range of other things. They would watch many, many lessons and would interview staff at length about how the school operates.

And next week the leader of the team would be visiting to talk to me and gain a first impression. Before then I had to fill in the most frightening form in a head's list of frightening forms, the S4. It was going to be a busy week and no, I wasn't going to go home feeling good tonight. I was going to let the staff know the bad news and then go home feeling crap!

Spring Term: Week 2

There's only one 'f' in Ofsted

A fearsome few days had passed. I had spent most of my time in the office with the door closed so that I could complete the dreaded S4. This form is a headteacher's self-evaluation of the school. In it, one has to give all the contextual information that an inspection team might want. A huge part of the form involves the head's views of the school's strengths and weaknesses and this puts one in something of a lose-lose situation. If I outlined any weaknesses I would be giving the inspectors something to get their teeth into before they even started. They would come looking for those weaknesses and use them against us in the final inspection report. If I outlined any strengths then I would have to be sure they were real, one hundred percent strengths. If the inspectors found any chinks of weakness in my 'strengths' then my judgement would be thrown into question. And yet I had to write pages and pages of information for the team to read. It was a little like writing the inspection report oneself and I didn't find it easy.

I had known schools to fail their inspections outright because of what had been written on the S4. The form had prejudged the inspection so that the team came in with an expectation that the school would be failing. I had known heads lose their jobs because their schools had failed their inspections. These people had written their own demise on that form and I didn't want to join their ranks. There was a local S4 going round some schools in the area that one head had filled in with the intention that others copy it. It was a nice idea but schools are too individual for it to have worked well.

I was not the only one in a state of panic. The entire staff had fallen into depression. Every member of staff was doubting their competence in the classroom, being full sure that the things they were proud of would be cruelly criticised by the inspectors. Many had memories of their last inspection just four years ago. The poor performance of one class, which contained eighteen children with special needs, came in for intense inspection. The teacher at the time responsible for the class was subjected to three and a half hours of solid observation for three days, followed by in-depth interviews at the end of each day in which she had to justify her credibility. At the end of the inspection the lady was a nervous wreck and whilst the inspectors had finally agreed that the class was made up of many non-academic children, the teacher resigned shortly afterwards and the school lost a talented member of its team.

Whilst the walls were now covered with fresh, new displays, the mood in school was black. Such tense situations always seem to emphasise the deeper personalities of individuals. As a result Gillian was now power-mad. She was aiming to control everything and everybody that passed within a mile of her and this did not impress the rest of the staff. Alan was more serious than ever. He didn't enjoy being watched and scrutinised. It was not a thing he did well and he was not looking forward to it at all. He did, however, have full confidence that his curriculum planning would be perfect. Jenny was hoarding like she'd never hoarded before, just to make sure she didn't run out of essential supplies during the inspection period.

And Walt had sensed the tension in the air. He had explained to me that he couldn't understand the panic because his urinals were currently in better condition than had been the case for two years. The inspectors, he concluded, were bound to be impressed by that. Walt had not been impressed, however, by the apparent ineptitude of the teaching staff. They had been parking badly in the car park and had been tidying their cupboards and throwing out more rubbish than he was expecting. This had a detrimental effect on his bin-filling routines and had caused him to need to order more bin liners. In respect of the car park, this had been a simple problem to solve. He had procured some yellow road paint and marked out a set of double yellow lines down one edge of the car park, thus ensuring that the area did not become crowded with abandoned vehicles.

And so Wednesday morning arrived and brought with it dark clouds and gusty winds. It was set to become far more of a miserable day because, at ten o'clock, I was due to receive my first visit from the Registered Inspector, Nigel Blackwell. Nigel would be the leader of the inspection team and, as is customary, he had arranged to make an introductory visit well ahead of the inspection. This was not, he had insisted on the telephone, part of the inspection and no judgements would be made. I believed him as much as I believed that the world was flat.

I had wanted to have a quiet morning in which to prepare for Nigel's visit but at nine-twenty I heard a commotion on the corridor. Stepping out of my office to investigate I found myself face to face with the Mad Woman who was shouting at Ann.

"Well, he's here now, so I can see him!" she snapped at Ann. "I need to see you and it's important!" she then snapped at me.

I explained that I didn't have very much time available but I would see her for a few minutes. She barged into my room and plonked herself heavily onto a swivelling office chair. The sudden pressure on this chair caused its gas lift to momentarily give up the fight and the seat sank to its lowest position, taking the Mad Woman with it and humorously trapping her foot between the seat base and the floor. She spent a moment grunting and attempting to gently lift her not inconsiderable posterior from the seat whilst still not being able to free her foot from its snare. She fell forward and the chair followed her. And from her new position on hands and knees on the office floor with a swivel chair draped over her arse she said, undaunted, "I've got a serious complaint!"

Her complaint was that 'Our Michael' had lost one of his trainers, a size four in white. Her view of the situation offered two simple scenarios. Either another child had taken this trainer, with the full knowledge of the teacher, of course, and had hidden this article in a secret place where all Michael's things are hidden. This secret place, she assumed, is known to everyone in the school except 'Our

Michael' so that much jollity and amusement can be gained from watching him search fruitlessly for lost items. The alternative version was that the teacher had confiscated this trainer and had subsequently lost it and this was now being made to look like 'Our Michael's' fault so that the school did not have to pay for another pair of trainers.

My suggestion that it could have been lost innocently was scorned indeed. I went on to explain that if he had taken it off, to change for a games lesson, it could have been accidentally kicked along the floor and ended up in another part of the classroom. She began to like this theory and within seconds she had decided that a group of children had indeed been kicking it around the room and had lost it. These children had therefore been guilty of bullying and they should be punished severely, she decided. But she assumed that the school would do nothing because it was only 'Our Michael' and so it didn't matter.

It was now nine-fifty and I could hear a car rumbling up the driveway. From my office window I saw a dark blue Saab stop at the edge of the car park and I noticed the man inside shuffling some papers. This was Nigel Blackwell, the inspector. I had to get rid of the Mad Woman but we were going round in circles. And then outside the window I saw Walt appear from nowhere and march over to the Saab. I stopped listening to the Mad Woman and struggled to hear Walt's exchange with our official Grim Reaper.

"Nah then! Have you passed your driving test or what, pal!" Walt began as he tapped on the window of the car. I couldn't make out the reply.

"Well you'll know what double yellow lines mean then, won't you. I've not put these here as a work o' bloody art. I've put 'em here to stop some bloody pancake parking on 'em and getting his car smacked when t'teachers reverse out. Get it shifted, nah then!"

Once again I could not make out the reply but common sense afforded me a fair assessment of what the possible response might be.

"I know t'bloody car park's full. It's always bloody full but you can't go parking here, not now I've put these yellow lines down. It's an elf and safety. You'll have to park out on t'road, pal. No, *you* listen to *me*! We've got a bloody inspector coming this morning and he'll be looking for elf and safetys. If the bugger turns up and finds you parked here we'll be off to a pisser of a start and I'll tell you that and I'll tell you now and when it's said it's said. So get it shifted!" There was a moment of quiet reflection out in the car park, which was followed by a softer, more restrained Walt responding with the phrase, "You're the what? *You* are? Shit! I'll leave it with you!" And with that parting 'shit', Walt walked away to categorise his nuts.

I was aware that I hadn't listened to a word that the Mad Woman had said for the last five minutes, but it didn't really matter, I already knew that everything was the school's fault and that 'Our Michael' was being perpetually picked on. I told her I'd look into the mystery of the missing trainer but that she really must go as I had an appointment right now. To my surprise, although still moaning, she stood up and headed for the door. I opened the door just as the inspector stepped onto the corridor. The Mad Woman, seeing the possibility of solidarity with what she perceived to be another parent, turned to the inspector and shouted, "I hope you're not expecting any answers from him! It's always the same at this place, they fob you off with rubbish! I know our Michael's being bullied and picked on, but do they care? They couldn't care less at this place. I've been in more times than I can remember and nothing gets done. It needs closing down, this place. Nice to meet you, good morning."

That woman had no idea what went on, day in, day out, behind the scenes at this and every other decent school. And all of it, all the efforts of a dedicated staff, was poised to go down the toilet because that infuriating idiot of a woman couldn't keep her mouth shut. I hated her with a passion at this point.

Attempting to make a fresh start with Nigel Blackwell, I greeted him, invited him into my office and offered him a coffee. He was about average height and sported black hair and a small, not quite Hitler-esque moustache. He wore a black suit with a white shirt and dark blue tie and could, to all intents and purposes have been about to attend a funeral. A niggling thought regarding the possibility that the said funeral could be mine was hard to push out of my mind. He eyed me with suspicion and rightly so. After all, in the few minutes since he arrived he had been set upon by my caretaker and then observed a parent shouting abuse about my school whilst I stood, in a stance reminiscent of Basil Fawlty, cheerily waving her off.

Nigel chose to launch straight into the business and for this I was grateful. "The purpose of this morning's visit is to collect the documentation from you and to get a general feel of the school." He began. "I tend, on these visits, to have an informal chat with the head and then visit the staff room so that I can 'a' meet the staff and 'b' let the staff see me. I shall also be requiring a lunch which I would like to eat with the children and yourself in the dining room. I trust your budget can run to providing me with lunch?" He smiled a rather sickly smile and took a sip of his coffee. "After that, a quick chance to meet your secretarial team and any other useful ancillaries would be appreciated. I asked for you to arrange for the Chair of Governors to be here, did you do that?

"He'll be here around lunch time." I replied.

"Ah, good. He can join us for lunch."

I buzzed through to Ann and asked her to order lunches for the three of us, to be paid for from the school budget, except mine as I would give her the money. The man was already grating on me and I was going to find it hard to remain civil to him. But I had to, and I kept reminding myself of that fact.

I picked up a two-foot high pile of documentation to hand over to Nigel. On my letter informing me of the inspection I had been given a list of policies, plans, contracts and financial information that was required as background. It had taken Ann two days to pull it all together and make relevant photcopies. This pile of documents, along with my completed S4 form, would determine the initial response of the inspection team. I handed it over with a sense of foreboding and uneasy finality.

When the morning break began, Nigel suggested that we stop discussing the documents for a while, which I was happy to do, and that we go and sit in the staff room, which I was less happy about. I felt a little guilty about invading the private space of the staff by depositing an Ofsted inspector there. The staff room was the one place where they could let off steam and be themselves and I expected nobody to thank me for bringing this particular visitor along. But none of that seemed to remotely concern Nigel as he burst through the door without knocking and positioned himself in an easy chair.

I introduced him to the members of staff who were already in the room and an uncomfortable silence replaced the earlier buzz of conversation. Two teachers suddenly remembered that they had something to do in their classrooms and everyone else wished they'd thought of that first. June, a classroom assistant, offered Nigel a cup of coffee and he declined this in a patronising manner, almost suggesting that she should be aware of the fact that he had just finished a drink in my office. She sat down, feeling that she had been chastised, and looked at the floor.

The silence continued. And then the door burst open and in walked Paul and Alan. Paul was in mid-conversation as he flung the door open. "…and he said, 'you don't spell it like that, there's only one 'f' in Ofsted.' And the other fellah said 'it's a bloody good job, nobody could cope if we had two effing Ofsteds!' What's everybody so quiet for? Ah." Paul smiled at the inspector. The inspector managed a supercilious grin and then looked disdainfully around the room.

The silence took hold once more and reigned for some time, only broken by the occasional uncomfortable slurp as someone misaligned their coffee cup with their mouth. Alan, never one to recognise the finer peculiarities of a situation, took a drink from his cup and then announced, "Quite nice to have a bit of silence isn't it!

I'm a lover of silence, it's a thing I enjoy. Surprising what you can hear when it's silent – birds singing, wind in the trees – of course you could argue that it technically isn't silent if you can hear things but there we go." No-one answered. "Soft music too!" he continued. "I'm a lover of soft music. Never liked loud stuff, can't think with loud stuff going on. I'm a lover of having a good think, it's a thing I do well. Often wish I'd learned to play an instrument but I don't have rhythm. Yes. Frere Jacques with one finger, my limit."

Nigel stared incredulously at Alan. It was the first time I'd felt any affinity with the inspector, but of the two, I still preferred Alan. And then the door opened and Walt's head appeared around it. The inspector flinched and Walt announced loudly, "Nah then, t'boys' bogs are buggered. We've gorra leak and you'll have to send all t'older lads to little uns' bogs. It's all over t'floor, the bugger. It's a pipe what's done it. A kid came and telled me and when he telled me I said it'll be a pipe what's done it and I had a look and I were right, it were a pipe what had done it. So if anybody wants me, I'll be incognito!" His final phrase had little meaning to the uninitiated but Walt no doubt had a good idea what he meant.

The end of the morning break brought about a sense of uncharacteristic relief as the staff had an excuse to leave the staff room. No doubt they would think it had been my idea to take the man in there and I would have to work hard to convince them otherwise. I didn't need morale to start failing at this point in the game.

Back in my office we sat down to talk. Nigel wanted me to give him a brief insight into my educational philosophy and my vision for the long term development of the school. He hoped this discussion would last around twenty minutes. In my current state of panic I feared that twenty seconds may be a more realistic goal. I began talking, as if being interviewed for a new job, but sitting in my own office. Within two minutes there was a loud bang on the door. Before I had the chance to see who was outside, the door opened and Matty Ward rushed in. Matty was a lovely, but rather frantic young man who had a severe speech impediment. And he clearly had something vital to tell me. "Thur, thur, tum twitly. Danny's got a big dick and he's waving it at people in der toilets!" he announced. The inspector's eyes widened in horror and I leapt to my feet in panic. Nigel followed me as I followed Matty along the corridor to the scene of the crime. Hardly knowing what to expect I pushed open the toilet door amidst the sound of giggling and squeals of delight.

Danny, a young man of seven and in foster care because his mother had dumped him at Social Services one night saying she was sick of him, was indeed in the toilets. And he did have something in his hand that really shouldn't have been there. It was, as Matty had tried to explain, a big stick which he must have found on the yard at break time. Entering a toilet had never given me so much relief. Whilst Danny needed to be reprimanded, I could relax in the knowledge that at least he did not need to be arrested. On any other day, I might have even found it amusing!

As we returned to my office the telephone was ringing. Ann had left her office and had gone to distribute various admin items around school and so I answered the phone.

"Hello, could I speak to Mr. Webb?" said a voice on the other end of the line.

"I'm sorry, there's no-one of that name here. You must have the wrong number." I replied.

"Oh, sorry. Goodbye." Said the man.

I put the phone down and tried to remember where I had left off in the discussion we were having before Danny and his big dick interrupted us. And then the phone rang again. The inspector looked disgruntled.

"Can I speak to Mr. Webb please?" said the voice on the other end of the line. It was the same voice as before.

"You've got the wrong number again, I'm sorry. You just rang this number a moment ago." I replied.

"Ah, sorry about that. I'll try not to do it again. Goodbye."

I replaced the handset and looked at Nigel. His face gave away no emotion. He raised his eyebrows and said, "Right, back to your vision for the school." I took a deep breath and prepared to start talking when the phone rang once more. Nigel eyed me with an air of derision, as if he truly believed that I had engineered this entire farce. I asked him to excuse me and I picked up the phone once again.

"I'm sorry," said the same voice as before, "can I speak to Mr. Jeffcock? *I'm* Mr. Webb."

"You're Mr. Webb? You've been ringing up and asking to speak to yourself! That's an expensive way to talk to yourself!"

"I'm sorry. I get nervous on the phone."

Mr. Webb explained that he had a child in school. The child was not called Webb because it had taken its mother's name of Riley. It had then changed to Beal when mum got a new boyfriend but reverted back to Riley when mum dumped him eight months later. Mr. Webb had not seen his child for two and a half years. Despite having unrestricted access to the boy, he often forgot to turn up for their meetings. But now he had been overcome with a burning desire to come into school and find out how the boy was getting along, because that is what good fathers do. I rapidly fixed up an appointment for him. He didn't write it down because he couldn't find a pen and his pencil had snapped, but he felt sure he would be able to remember it. I had less confidence in this than Mr. Webb had. But my gut feeling was rather stupidly based on the fact that he had merely telephoned the school and asked to speak to himself and I was probably being a little hard on the man.

The inspector was clearly agitated. But Mr. Webb had given me a new outlook on the situation. I was now quite angry that Nigel Blackwell was so put out by the fact that I was doing my job and speaking to an estranged parent. I was annoyed that he felt more important than Mr. Webb, who may have been plucking up the courage to ring me for seven months but kept copping out or forgetting. And what about the poor Webb-Riley-Beal-Riley child? What could an inspection do to improve the lot of a kid who suffered a name change more often a dodgy nuclear power station? Didn't he need a bit of security? Instead, the teachers were in a state of panic and giving no real attention whatsoever to the children. I was ready to philosophise and be visionary and Nigel would wonder what had hit him.

The smell of food drifted down the corridor and signalled to me that lunch time was approaching. I had talked for thirty-five minutes about my views on what education has become rather than what it ought to be. I had explained my distrust of people who sit in offices and churn out convenient statistics without understanding any of the issues behind them. I may have also mentioned what a bloody waste of time inspections are, based on my view that when they are over, the staff are too knackered to put any effort into their teaching for at least a term and this negates any benefits that preparation for an inspection might have had. I also believe I told him that it was not necessary to spend thirty-thousand pounds on inspecting a school – it would have the same effect if the government spent the price of a stamp, on a letter saying that the school *might* be inspected soon. The resultant savings could pay for an extra teacher so that a real difference could be made. He didn't seem to like that comment.

The sound of children in the hall told me that lunch time had now arrived and with it came the Chair of Governors. He was waiting in the corridor as Nigel and I walked to the hall for lunch. I introduced the two to each other and suggested we collected our meal before we tried to have a conversation. Lorna, the dinner lady supervising the queue of children looked suspiciously at the three of us as we entered the hall.

"Lorna, this is our Chair of Governors and this is Nigel Blackwell. Nigel will be leading the inspection team." I informed her. She was unused to being in such exalted company and was clearly overcome. She performed a curtsey and blurted out the phrase, "Very pleased to meet you Mr. Government and Mr. Inspector." Nigel enjoyed this level of deference and revelled in it. "I hope you like your lunch." Lorna continued, "it's Chicken Teddies and peas with a choice of potatoes. Chicken Teddies are pieces of chicken shaped like teddy bears. There's sponge and custard as well. I've never met an inspector before and it's nice to meet you. Enjoy your lunch." She backed away from him and curtseyed once more and then, to his surprise, let out a roar at the children which proved a danger to the ear drums, "Shurrup the lot of yer! Yer mekkin too much row and yull upset t'inspector. Nah shurrup!"

The visitors picked up a plastic 'flight tray' and began walking to the serving counter. The Chair of Governors was suffering a mixed set of emotions. On one hand he was feeling very important to have been included in this preliminary discussion but on the other, he was as nervous as hell. This was evidenced when Nigel began to speak to him as they approached the counter. The Chair spun round to answer at lightning speed and in so doing, flung his tray into the face of a six year old girl. The girl sustained a nose bleed and on seeing the blood dripping to the floor, began to scream with vigour. Lorna appeared, quick as a flash, and rammed a paper towel into the child's face whilst simultaneously asking, "Who did that? Have they been messing with these blinking trays again? Show me who did it, duck, and they can miss their playtime." The dripping girl pointed to the Chair of Governors who responded with the phrase, "Ah! Ah! Bit of an accident there. Is she alright?" The man's lack of observation skills had clearly reached new depths. Asking if a small child, who has a sliced cheek and a bleeding nose after being set upon by an adult, is alright was rather pointless in my view. And as Lorna took the child to the first aid box, I gleefully turned to the chair and suggested, "When her mum comes in to complain tonight, I wonder how she'll react when I tell her that her daughter was belted by the Chair of Governors!"

"It was clearly an accident!" he spluttered.

"Mmm. But I seem to remember once dealing with a vicious attack on your daughter...Perhaps I should permanently exclude you!"

"Message received." He replied.

We sat down to eat. Each table seated eight people, three along each side and one at each end. Nigel sat at the end and the Chair and I sat either side of him. Children, who stared intensely at the two men, took the rest of the seats. Nigel, having worked in education for many years was used to being surrounded by children but the Chair, being a prat, dealt with the situation badly. On seeing a pair of seven year olds looking at him, he greeted them.

"Afternoon." He said. "Enjoying your lunch?" The two children giggled and sniggered. One went so far as to permit the orange juice she was drinking dribble out of the corner of her mouth as she laughed. Aware that they were still looking at him, he attempted to draw them into conversation once more. "I like these chicken bear things. Do you like them?" The two girls giggled once more and then one whispered to the other. The 'whisperee' then looked at the Chair and laughed. "My friend says you're fat!" She announced. Not expecting this response, the Chair replied, "Well, I have to watch the tum, but I'd rather not talk about it here."

"Who are you anyway?" one of the girls asked.

"I'm the Chair." Said the Chair with devastating accuracy.

The girls sprayed their drinks across the table as they laughed. "He's a chair!" they said to each other. "How can you be a chair? You've not got four legs!"

"No, no, you're misunderstanding me. I'm not a chair like the chair you're sitting on…"

"Cos that's got four legs!" the girl replied.

"No, I'm a Chair-man."

"Do people sit on you, then?"

"No, no. Let me explain the details of governance…"

Fortunately for the girls, he never attained this conversational height. Instead, a nine-year-old boy walked by with his shoelaces dangling freely. As he became adjacent to the inspector, he tripped over the aforementioned dangly bits and for the second time in a short period, a plastic tray was to become an uncontrollable weapon. This time, however, the tray contained food. At least it did at the point when it left the boy's grasp. The tray itself injured no-one on this occasion but the trajectory of its contents was the cause of much merriment. On hearing the crash as the tray hit the floor, every child in the hall stopped talking and stopped eating. They looked to the scene of the accident. The tray was of little consequence to them but the man sitting next to its point of contact with the floor had become an object of fascination. The man in question was Nigel Blackwell. Custard was dripping down the side of his face and trickling onto his lapels. The accompanying sponge had lodged itself a little way above his left ear but looked set to move imminently. Mashed potato had settled on his lap and peas were scattered variously around his anatomy. A chicken teddy protruded from his jacket pocket and his shirt was now a very trendy shade of 'blackcurrant white'.

Celia and Alma chose this moment to walk through the hall on their way to the staff room. Looking across to where we were sitting, their faces said everything I wanted to say. I smiled at them and they set off quickly to pass on the news to the rest of the staff. I assumed that all would be distraught to hear of the nice man's fate.

Walt appeared faster than the speed of smell, equipped with a mop, bucket and brush. He stood and looked at the inspector. "I'll tell you this and I'll tell you now and I'll tell you reight and straight and when it's said it's said and I'll say no more. Your credibility's gone right through t'window pal! Stand up and I'll help you get cleaned up." Nigel stood up and Walt proceeded to prod at him with a sweeping brush. The Chair of Governors remained firmly seated, sporadically repeating the phrase, "Ah, ah!"

Walt looked at the mess around him. "It's a reight mess and no mistake, this is. I'll have to mop it and leave it to dry. It's an elf and safety, this, so you'll need to keep these 'ere kids away from it." He looked at Nigel. "You look like an elf and safety yourself, pal. Have you brought a change of clothes, no you won't have will you! I'll lend you a spare boiler suit seeing as how you can't walk round looking like a mobile pizza. You'll have to let me have it back though. I can't be giving boiler suits away."

Nigel left, having had little chance to converse with the Chair of Governors. He looked dapper in Walt's spare burgundy boiler suit but insisted on sniffing it at regular intervals and then looking nauseous. He took away his pile of documentation and promised Walt that the outfit would be returned.

I decided that tomorrow morning I would, as usual play some music on the CD player as the children walked into the assembly. Tomorrow, there was only one choice of song. Tomorrow the children would listen to 'The Only Way Is Up'.

Spring Term: Week 3

Walt claimed to have only a very basic knowledge of computers but he was certain that they should neither send out smoke signals, nor burst into flames.

Badness had been committed in the boys' toilets. I was informed of this by Walt, mid-way through Tuesday morning, after a thorough urinal inspection had taken place.

"Come and look at this, nah then!" Walt insisted. I dropped my budget forecasts and followed Walt into the toilet. He somewhat disconcertingly closed the door behind us, resulting in our being rather trapped in a confined space together. Already, I was longing for the aroma of cool, fresh air. However, the reason he had chosen to close the door was to show me what at first appeared to be ancient, intricate Neolithic carvings of indeterminate shape on the inside of the wooden door. And then I realised that some kids had tried to display the names of their favourite football teams on the door using a sharp instrument.

"I'd like to know what little prick's done that, nah then!" he commented.

"I think it's more likely to be a pair of scissors or something, Walt." I replied.

"I'll leave it with you! But you want to find out who did it or else you'll be having graphology everywhere. And I won't be cleaning it off, I'll tell you that and I'll tell you now."

The toilet was used by the boys from the oldest two year groups and so it was likely that the culprit could be tracked down quite easily. Nevertheless, I decided to visit the two classes and apply a little pressure. On entering Alan's class, I apologised for interrupting and then told the children to listen.

"Someone has been vandalising the boys' toilet door." I began. There was a collective gasp, not through genuine concern, but simply because most children thought this would look good and deflect any suspicion from them. "Somebody's been carving into the door and I'm not happy about it. You can't paint over deep grooves that somebody's carved. We'll probably need a new door. And the money for buying a new door and having it fitted has to come out of money that we should be spending on other things, like books or CD

Roms. Now I'm going to find out who did this and there are two ways I can get an answer. The best way would be for whoever did it to come and see me some time today. That would be very mature and you may well be in a lot less trouble. But there is another way. The security cameras around school – and no, there aren't any in the toilets, don't worry – the security cameras point towards entrance doors. There's one across the courtyard pointing right at your corridor. If I look at the tape, somebody – probably a little group of somebodies – will have taken an unusually long time between going in to the toilets and coming back out again. Later today I intend to look, if I haven't had any information from the person who did the carving."

I didn't mention that the cameras were never on in the daytime, or that the system had been knackered since November and wouldn't work again until we could afford to fix it. Those points, I concluded, were superfluous to my argument.

"Vandalism!" said Alan. "Not an advisable thing. Makes such a mess. I'm not a lover of mess, it's messy. Costs money too, vandalism, not mess. Wasting money is such a, well, waste of money. Need to own up if you did it. Nothing worse than a crook who's also dishonest. Well, most crooks are dishonest because what they do is not exactly, well, honest, but you get my drift. Yes, carry on with your work."

Alan, clearly proud of his speech, gave me a contented nod as I left the room.

I resolved to wait until later in the day and then go back to threaten the watching of the video if nobody had come forward. But before that time, I had a meeting to attend. The meeting was to discuss the progress of the building work. It was also to be attended by the contractor, Rob the Architect and a man called Simon who was the project manager for the LEA. They assembled in my office at ten-fifteen.

It appeared that Simon, who had worked with lots of extensions to schools, was under the impression that this particular job was moving too slowly. In the ten or eleven weeks since the builders had arrived they were just completing the concrete foundations. The projected timescale of sixteen weeks was looking decidedly wide of the mark.

"We've hit problems with the ground." The contractor protested.

"You should have allowed for that." Simon replied. "It took two weeks for you to get a structural engineer to tell you how to sort out the crumbling rock. You were supposed to have tendered for the job *after* reading the survey notes. You should have known you'd need to underpin it."

"Yes but…"

"And you've not been getting things delivered on time. Your men have been sitting there idle because materials haven't been delivered. And we're paying for this. I think it's time to start considering financial penalties if you don't sort your act out."

"Hold on!" said the contractor. "There's no need to be hasty."

"I think you've proved that admirably!" quipped Simon, rather impressively.

Simon complained that this project was becoming a bit of an embarrassment from a PR point of view. I asked if we could perhaps be presented with a plaque to join all the other awards on the wall of the entrance hall. This one could say, 'Hilltop Primary School has been declared an Official Embarrassment' but nobody took up the offer. The contractor explained that things hadn't gone well on the ordering and delivery front because they were having their office decorated and so they were in a bit of turmoil. At this point I chose to explode, pointing out that having half the playground dug up, two of the four exit doors permanently blocked and incessant lorries driving across what was left of the yard, I believed we were in just a little more turmoil. He got my drift.

It was decided that a site inspection was necessary and we duly left my office and ventured out to look at the progress for ourselves. The builders were busily smoothing off the concrete that had been poured out of a lorry previously. This was to form a level base on which to begin the brickwork. Suddenly, as I was lost in thought about something entirely unrelated, I heard someone call out the familiar phrase, "Get off that, you daft twat!" As expected, the poet was a builder and the daft twat in question was Simon. He had walked along one of the newly smoothed concrete foundation bases, much to the chagrin of Mick, the foreman.

"You soft nonk!" said Mick, rushing over to where Simon was wiping cement off his shoes. "What yer bloody doing on here anyway?"

Simon explained who he was and Mick grinned. "Ey lads!" he shouted, "This is Simon. It's Simon who I telled yer about."

"Drain Man!" the builders shouted in unison.

Puzzled by the apparent knowledge the builders already had about Simon, I wandered casually over to Mick and asked him to supply a little more detail. He was happy to do so. "Walt's warned us about this wanker!" he began. "He's supposed to go round schools and check up on building work and look at what might need doing in t'future. Sounds like when he leaves a place, there's a damn sight more that needs doing than before he came. Walt told us how he were in charge of this new nursery project at a school in town. And because they were building it down to a price it were his job to make sure no corners were being cut. Anyway, he missed something. They'd saved money by allowing t'foul water drainage to drop into a soakaway and he never spotted it on t'plans. So every time some bugger flushed t'bog, everything went down a short pipe that ended under t'school field. After a couple of years there were people complaining about this horrible smell coming from t'field. They dug down and found two years worth of shit underground and backing up t'pipe. He were responsible for that!"

"For the drain, not for the two years worth of shit, I assume!"

"I'm not so sure. He's full of it from what I've heard."

Our conversation was curtailed because Simon was once again the subject of the builders' wrath. He had decided to poke vigorously at some concrete that had already set. The reasons for his actions were unclear to all but the point of issue centred around the object he had chosen as a 'poking instrument'. It was a screwdriver, obtained from the edge of the site. The owner of this instrument was less than pleased to see it being used thus.

"That's mine, that is. Put it down before I ram it up yer arse!" he suggested

"I want to check the…" Simon began.

"Not wi'my twatting screwdriver, you don't. I have to pay for my tools, pal. And I'm not having some bugger busting it. Now put it down or you'll be part of these bloody foundations!"

Simon saw sense and stopped messing with the nice man's tool. This was a relief to everybody.

During Simon's little adventure with the screwdriver, none of us had taken much notice of a delivery lorry at the far end of the playground. The playground ended at a tall wire fence and the area directly beyond it was technically still part of the school premises, sometimes used as an overflow car park. It had a big shrub in the middle of it which Walt was one day going to remove. We had

agreed with the builders that, when they were onto the groundwork,

a little extra hardcore and the creative use of a JCB could make the

area into quite an acceptable parking zone, as opposed to the muddy

one it now was. Today, no cars were parked there. We had asked

everyone to leave the area clear so that a delivery of one and a half

inch stone could be deposited there. The builders needed this

throughout their work and so an entire lorry-load had been ordered.

As Mick signed the lorry driver's papers and waved him off,

Simon pointed at the vehicle and said, "He's just tipped a full load of

stone behind that fence!" We agreed that Simon had made an

accurate observation and began to look again at the building work.

"But I can't get my car out now!" he said.

Everybody went quiet. Without saying a word, we walked to

the fence and stared. Simon had tucked his car neatly behind the big

shrub. His green Vauxhall Vectra had blended perfectly with its

surroundings, being an identical shade to the shrub. And the lorry

had tipped a huge pile of stone at the other side of the shrub, totally

blocking Simon's exit. Imagining from my recent conversation with

Mick that Simon preferred exits to be open and unrestricted, I assumed this situation might not be exactly to his liking.

Walt's yellow Jeep came rocketing up the drive. He had been on a maintenance mission, satisfying the need to augment his impressive cache of buckets. He parked and came over to us. "They've delivered it then, nah then."

"Yes they have Walt." I confirmed. It would have been difficult to not confirm his statement as the pile of stone was five and a half feet high and rather obvious, even to the casual observer. "There's just one little problem."

"Problem? It looks alright to me. I'll tell you this and I'll tell you now, it's decent stone that is."

"There's nothing wrong with the stone. It's the car parked behind it that's bothering us." I explained.

Walt walked round the side of the fence and spotted the car. "Well bugger me backwards! What bloody pancake's gone and parked there? We said nobody were to park there! And even if they did, how bloody stupid do you have to be to hide the bugger behind t'foliage? Do we know whose it is?"

Simon gave an embarrassed cough. "It's mine." He mumbled.

Walt, not being one of Simon's greatest fans, fell headlong into a fit of laughter from which it was going to take a long time to recover.

"I don't know how to get it out." Simon whined.

"Well there aren't many options, as I see it!" Walt exclaimed. "You can't pick it up and carry it out, we've sold t'helicopter so we can't lift it out and you're not likely to be driving over that pile as it stands now. I'll lend you mi barrow!"

"Your barrow? What…"

"Well I'm not lending it you to ride home on! It's for shifting t'stone. I can't see no other way out, can you! I'll leave it with you!"

With the barrow duly delivered, the meeting was declared closed. The men who had attended the meeting all had to leave in a hurry, the builders had work to do and Walt had a date with his favourite urinal. I felt I should stay and help Simon in his hour of need. On his own, it might become closer to a week of need! I moved one shovel-full of stone and was rescued by Ann. She needed me to come urgently to the office. There was a major problem.

I couldn't decide whether to be happy or apprehensive. It might be that Walt had primed her but the urgency in her voice sounded a little too convincing for that. The alternative might be an aggressive parent who wanted to do less than pleasant things to me for reasons thus far unknown. I would have to wait until I was close enough for her to tell me.

It was neither. Ann's computer had started smoking, she informed me. Smoke was being emitted from the back of the CPU and she wasn't altogether sure that this was right. Walt had seen it and had informed her that it indeed wasn't right. He claimed to have only a very basic knowledge of computers but this was enough to be certain that the buggers should neither send out smoke signals, nor burst into flames. Ann was quite convinced by his argument and had resolved to include me in the forthcoming explosion.

It was still smoking when we reached her office.

"Have you unplugged it?" I asked her.

"No, I wanted you to see for yourself so you knew what the smoke looked like." She proudly stated.

"I'd have believed you, Ann. Let's get it unplugged." I reached for the plug and Ann yelled, "No! Don't!" Jumping back in a panic, I looked for a reason for Ann's sudden burst of energy.

"I've got to shut it down first. They told me on the training course. I'm never to switch it off without shutting it down first. It can damage the something-or-other." she explained.

"So can the bloody thing bursting into flames. I think on this occasion we can forget shutting down. Let's just get the thing off."

"Will that be OK?"

"Ann, we're well beyond OK!"

I asked Ann to phone the LEA and tell them exactly what happened, from the moment she realised something was wrong. I should never have used the word 'exactly'.

"Hello, it's Ann at Hilltop Primary here." She said. "I think we need someone to come out and help us with our computer in the office. Well dear, I was doing my work this afternoon, paying some invoices and things. Hasn't the price of paper gone up! Twenty boxes of A4 costs… oh right, yes. I was paying my invoices, you know, all the 'put the net price here and click here for the VAT and then check that it balances' and, ooh I hate it when you get some items that have VAT and some that don't, it gets me in a terrible tizzy, and…oh, sorry. Well anyway dear, I was on my own because the Head was outside with the architect. It's going ever so slowly, the new classroom. They won't finish it until…oh I do keep being sidetracked, don't I! Right, well, I was paying my invoices when I noticed smoke. It was coming from the back of the computer and there was more than you'd expect. Well, I suppose you wouldn't expect *any* really, but even if you did expect some, this was more. What did I do? I showed the caretaker and then I went to get the Head from outside. Oh yes, I've switched it off now. Do you think it'll be alright after it's cooled down? No, alright, you'll send a man out. What? What have I got on the computer? Well I don't put anything on it dear. It's not level on the top of the screen thingy so there's nothing on it. No there's no programmes on it, it isn't connected up to the aerial. Oh, I see. Oh you must think I'm dizzy, it's got all the usual LEA disks in it and a word processing thingy. What dear? Do I put what on it? Spreadsheets? No, I used to cover it over with an old drape but I've stopped doing that since we had the new blinds fitted. No I don't think it's helping either, you don't seem to be asking me the right questions. Good, he'll be here tomorrow morning. I'll not switch it on for now then. Bye dear."

She put the phone down and smiled contentedly. "Glad that's sorted out." She said. "I'll get those letters done now. Oh, I can't, can I! I'll make a drink then!"

Out in the playground, Simon was shovelling stones at a frantic pace in an attempt to clear a path for his car to drive through. Walt, surprisingly, had joined him and was helping things along by leaning on the spare shovel and offering observations about the world in general, and pancakes more specifically. As I approached, Walt left his shovel and came across to me.

"I see you're giving him a hand then Walt!" I said sarcastically.

"Only hand I'd give him would have a red-hot bloody poker in it!" he responded, clearly having formed a bond with the man.

"So why have you come out to chat to him, if you dislike him so much!" I asked.

"I'll tell you this and I'll tell you now and I'll tell you reight and straight and when it's said it's said and I'll say no more, nah then. When he's been out to this school in t'past, he's bored me rigid wi' his dreary bloody voice. And I have to listen to him on account of him being big in school maintenance. He's like a boss, in a way. So now I've got the bugger. He's not going anywhere till he can get his car out from behind these stones and I'm telling him as many boring stories as I can remember. Not that I'm as boring as he is. People say I'm a good storyteller, but I can at least try to get my own back. Nah then."

A devious operator indeed, was Walt. Perhaps this was part of his mystique, the reason why he was such a babe magnet. Or was that a fly trap?

"You see," he suddenly continued, "he's only got one topic of conversation. Buildings. That's all he can talk about. He carps on about wall ties, flashings, soffits and all these other building things but he can't talk about nowt else. Nah then. Well if there's one thing about me it's this, and I'll tell you now. I can talk about anything to anybody. I'm multilingual, like. It's what makes people like me."

"Absolutely right, Walt. Which reminds me, what did you think to Ann's computer starting to smoke at such a young age?"

"Well, it's down to how they're maintained and that's not maintained well. Not like my urinals. Now I defy anybody to find fault with them, they're spotless…"

I made an excuse and left Walt to try out his wide range of conversations on Simon once more.

Immersed in my work I hardly noticed lunch time approach and so it was with a degree of surprise that the raucous laughter of the dinner ladies ventured into my eardrums quite so soon. Their laughter was interspersed by words such as 'car', 'pile of stones' and 'and now it's stuck on top'. Considering the latter phrase rather odd, I left what I was doing and went back to the area where Simon had been incarcerated for the last hour and a half. The sight that met me was a curious one. He had reduced the pile of stones to some degree but had now chosen to position his car on top of those that remained. And it was now stuck.

He looked embarrassed as I approached. Walt was already with him and was explaining the situation to him.

"He's a bloody pancake!" was his overriding feeling about the current position. "I were just telling him some unusual facts about sanitary fittings, to pass the time, like, and then he suddenly says 'that's it, I'm off' and he gets into his car and tries to drive it over what's left of this pile of stones, the bloody arsehole. I mean, it takes a bloody pancake to try and drive a car over a mountain of unrestrained aggregate, nah then!"

"I thought I'd be able to clear it." Simon explained. "It's only about nine inches high."

"Aye, well, you didn't, did you! There's blokes what have come to grief wi' less than nine inches and I'll tell you that, nah then! What's happened here is your wheels have dug down into this here pile. They've dug down, see. And now you've grounded your bloody car. It's your wheels that have done it. They're stuck, you see. You'll not get that shifted in a hurry. You see, you've got to start digging these here stones out from round your wheels now and that'll be a job and a half. You're well-wedged and that's a fact. I'd offer to help you except as I don't want to."

"I'll have to cancel my appointments for the day. I'm supposed to visiting three more schools this afternoon." Simon moaned.

"That'll be a pisser for 'em and no mistake!" Walt conceded. "I don't know what they'll do if you're not there to bugger up their buildings. Nobody can do it as well as you can. I'll tell you this and I'll tell you now, I shall be interested to hear what excuse you come up with."

"I'll have to try and come up with something that sounds realistic."

"How about, 'I'm a bloody daft pancake and I've driven me car up a pile of hardcore and got it stuck on top'. It's not quite as good as 'I've decided to let all that nursery's shit collect under t'school field' but I'll leave it with you. Anyway, I've got an appointment with a toilet."

"I thought you'd polished your urinals today, Walt!" I interrupted.

"I'm not cleaning the bugger, I need a piss!" And off he trotted.

Simon smiled pathetically. "I couldn't stand it any longer. I was desperate to escape. That man has got to be the most lavatorially obsessed being on the planet. He couldn't understand that I just don't give a damn about who he'd like to see eating out of them. And when he started even describing the meals he'd provide it just made me feel ill. Besides that, there was a funny smell that was turning my stomach. You perhaps ought to get the Environmental Health people to take readings of the air pollution. Anyway, I seized my chance and made a dash for it. I thought if I went at it quick enough I could get over to the other side. I misjudged it."

"Come and have a drink. If you like, you can sip it out of urinal number three!" I suggested.

He didn't even raise a smile.

By early afternoon, Simon's car had been the object of hilarity for every child on the playground but was now nearing ground level and looked set to touch down within the hour. Whilst the vehicle was not damaged, Simon's pride and reputation had been all but written off. From this point forward he would not be able to visit any school in the area without being reminded of the day he spent first trapped behind, and then stuck atop, a pile of hardcore. And if he chose to not respond to the jibes, the phrase 'stony silence' would no doubt enter the conversation.

I had almost forgotten two items on my list of things to do. The first was that I had promised to lend a video to Jenny. The video was a history programme that was relevant to the work her class was doing. I had recorded it a few years ago as a classroom teacher and had kept it because it was good. The second job was to inform a child in Alan's class that his mother wanted him to go to his granny's straight from school.

I picked up my video, in its plain, white box and set off through school. Alan's room was first on my route and I opened the door to find the class sitting in silence whilst Alan talked at them. This was something he did well. Before I had the chance to speak, three boys with dubious hairstyles looked in horror at an area in the vicinity of my crotch. Within seconds I was relieved to find that they were not inspecting my personal attributes but were instead looking at the box in my hand. They were clearly under the impression that I was delivering a security tape into their midst. Without any prompting, they suddenly shouted 'It was us, we did it!'

I stifled a smirk and Alan, catching up with the event, looked at the boys and said, "Well done boys, I'm very proud of you. Well, I'm not proud of you for damaging the toilet doors in the first place. No, horrible thing to do, not good at all. But proud of you for admitting it. Goes a long way, honesty. I've said it before and I'll say it again, honesty lets people know you're, er, honest. Yes. Dishonesty, it's a bad thing. Can't trust a dishonest person. No-one can, you know. I'm a real lover of honesty. Feel strongly about it." He turned to me and asked, "Are we going to watch the video?"

"No, I don't think we need to now." I answered. "I'll see you boys in my office at break time and we'll discuss punishments." I pulled Alan to one side and spoke quietly. "I came in here to give someone a message. This video is for Jenny, it's a history programme."

Alan let out a monstrous guffaw. "Bravo! Never get away with it myself! Can't fool anyone. It's not a thing I do well. End up in an awful mess if I did that. Better not mention honesty any more, though! Wonderful!"

I left Alan to pass on the message that I was supposed to have delivered. I would meet the two miscreants at break time and, because they had been honest, I would let them suggest their own punishments. They would think I was being kind. But when children choose their own punishments, they are always ridiculously hard on themselves and end up with far worse than a teacher would have chosen. And when their parents try to complain about it, I simply have to explain that I thought it was a little harsh but the children insisted. You learn to work the system in this, just as any other job!

And so ended another day of unexpected happenings. It had been a day in which a young computer had taken up smoking, a vandalism fraternity had been exposed and the senior buildings manager had got 'stoned' on school premises. Never mind, at least we had an inspection to look forward to.

Spring Term: Week 4

The phrase 'bollocks, I'm so bloody embarrassed' had been invented specifically for this moment

It dawned on me halfway through Tuesday morning that we had not had a fire drill during this term. The elf and safety regulations stated clearly that a rather unfortunately termed 'evacuation procedure' must be rehearsed once per term. The details of this should be noted down in a 'fire log' which should be created by the Headteacher. I was always glad to have never misread this instruction and attempted instead to create a log fire. The resultant conflagration may have caused me to wish we had recently had a fire drill. The details to be entered in the fire log included the date and time of the drill, along with the total evacuation time. Curiously, we were also encouraged to add 'other comments' in the log.

In my previous school I had held fire drills at difficult times, such as during whole-school assemblies or even during a lunch break. I had always argued a real fire might not wait until all the children were seated neatly at their desks before it broke out. I wanted to know how we would cope in a real emergency, when children were scattered all over the school and the playground. I had even been known to lock one of the exit doors and claim 'that's where the fire is, find another way out'. Such a move was always interesting.

But today was going to be a standard fire drill. Everyone would assemble on the playground to be registered and then we would go back inside and get on with what we were doing. Nobody wanted to waste too much lesson time with the inspectors coming next week, but equally, we needed to have the drill logged down in the book. So I went to tell Ann the good news.

I found her in her office, catching up with some bulk photocopying. Her computer was still at the dry cleaners and she was a very happy lady without it. "Ann, I'm going to do a fire drill." I said.

"Right. Shall I go round school and warn everybody?" she asked.

"No. Remember the one last term? I told you we shouldn't warn people. We should treat it like an actual fire. It's the only way we can get a real picture of the situation."

"Yes, but I still think it's a bit tricky trying to get three hundred children out when they're all panicking."

"That's the whole point. One day we might have to do it for real. We need to know the pitfalls."

"Yes, I suppose so. Do you want the kitchen staff out as well?"

"Everybody!"

"Only they never used to bother when the last head was here. It got in the way of their food preparation."

"Well bearing in mind that a fire's more likely to start in the kitchen than anywhere else, I want them to join us."

"Right. When the alarm rings, I'll go and tell them."

I picked up a stopwatch, switched it on and pressed the fire bell button. A piercing, shrill alarm reverberated throughout the school and within seconds I could hear the sound of movement all around the building. I held onto the button for a minute or so and then set off on a quick sweep of the school to see that no-one was still inside and that all the doors had been closed as they should be. Within another minute I was outside, observing all the teachers calling a register for their classes. It had been very successful. Nobody had panicked, nobody had been trampled to death – or even to near death – and everyone was calmly waiting to be sent back inside.

That was the point when the first wave of panic swept over me. All the external doors were fitted with strong door closers so that they slammed shut. They were also equipped with security locks in the wake of the awful attacks that have taken place in some schools across the country. Such locks are a perfect deterrent to intruders in that they operate with an ordinary door handle from the inside but require the use of a key in order to gain access from the outside. And as I fumbled frantically in my pocket I became acutely aware that I had not brought my key outside with me.

"Gillian! Got your key with you?" I asked. "I think I've left mine inside."

"My key? Oh, the one for the school doors? No it's in my handbag in the classroom."

I glanced around at the female staff and became uncomfortably hot as I realised that not a single one of them had a handbag attached to their body. So I wandered over to Alan and Paul who were wondering why we were all still standing outside. "You've, er, not got your school keys on you, have you chaps?" I asked with a smile.

"I've lost mine." Paul said.

"Got mine!" said Alan with a proud look on his face.

"Can I borrow it for a minute. I've not brought mine out with me."

"Ah, when I said 'got mine', I meant, haven't lost it." Alan explained. "Didn't mean, got it with me. On a hook behind my desk. Always keep it there. Never know when I might need it."

And so it went on. I asked Ann who was quite confident that she had never had one but she would have brought it out if she had. Diane the cook had definitely got hers and it was in her coat pocket. This was hanging up with the rest of her coat in the kitchen. The only other person who might have one was Walt, but he was on his break and had left the premises.

This struck me as something of a problem. We now had more than three hundred children and thirty-four adults standing on the school playground with no obvious means of gaining entry to the building. The phrase 'bollocks, I'm so bloody embarrassed' had been invented specifically for this moment, I decided.

I called the staff together and told them the rather intriguing news, suggesting that we should let the children have a break time for the moment whilst I tried to solve the problem.

"I'm sure it won't take too long to sort things out." I lied. "I don't suppose anyone's got their mobile phone out here, have they? I could ring Walt and ask him to come back early from his break."

Alan had got his mobile phone in his trouser pocket. He produced it with a flourish and smiled through his beard.

"So that's what the bulge is!" Amanda chortled. "I always knew they were wrong!"

"Yes, bit uncomfortable at times. Sometimes forget to turn the vibrate-alert off." Alan announced, utterly out of touch with the direction the conversation was heading.

"Whatever makes you happy!" Amanda said.

"Disconcerting at times, not to mention damned uncomfortable. But, always like to have it to hand. I'm a lover of having things to hand. Always make sure I do. It's a thing I do well."

Everybody wanted to make the joke, but nobody did. There were children about and one of them had a beard and mobile phone.

Alan began to pass his phone to me but stopped before I could reach it.

"Switched off!" he exclaimed. "Don't normally switch it off! Wonder when I did that… ah, battery's flat. Got a phone like you wanted, doesn't work. I don't usually let that happen. I'm very efficient with my batteries. It's a thing I do well. Check them regularly, every couple of nights. Must have forgotten. I'm a lover of routine usually. Get out of a routine, end up in the shit, that's what I always say. Well, not always! Say other things as well, but you get my drift."

"Your phone is dead, Alan. That's all I need to know." I said.

He put it back in his pocket and I could tell Amanda really, really wanted to make a crack about the bulge in his trousers being dead. She refrained and smiled to herself.

"You could go up to the shops and ring from there." Gillian suggested. That was actually a good idea and I set off to walk up the school drive and about a quarter of a mile up the road to the little row of shops. It took just over ten minutes. The row of shops consisted of a newsagent's, a chip shop, a hairdressing salon and a mini-market. There was a phone box on the pavement and I walked gleefully towards it.

It was a Phonecard call box. I had never owned a phone card in my entire life and consequently it was of no use to me. But I didn't feel concerned. I could go into a shop and borrow a phone. All was not lost. The chip shop was not open yet and so that reduced my list of possibilities to three. The hairdressing salon didn't seem appropriate because there might be someone's mum in there and I really didn't relish the comments that could be made. The mini-market seemed a little too busy. I suspected they might not be overjoyed at having to let me into the back of the shop when they had a queue of customers waiting at the till. And so I settled on the newsagent's. It was a spacious place, not terribly busy and probably very amenable, I assumed.

The girl behind the counter had a nice smile and this made me feel that the encounter would be successful.

"Could I use your phone?" I asked. "I wouldn't ask normally, but it's a bit of an emergency."

"Oh dear. Is someone hurt."

"No. Listen, actually I'm from the school. We've had a fire drill and we've all gone out without a key. We can't get back in and I need to ring the caretaker."

"Oops! I'm sure it'll be alright. Let me just check with my boss." She said. She went into the back of the shop and began talking to someone. Suddenly a roar of laughter bellowed through the shop and from behind the wall came her boss. His name was Mr. Price. I knew that because his son, David, was a pupil at the school. I had no particular liking for the boy and I now realised that this was because he suffered from hereditary obnoxiousness.

"Well that's a blinder!" were his opening words. "That's one to tell my customers. Is everybody locked out? Well I suppose they must be, cos you wouldn't be here wanting to use my phone otherwise would you! Are you going to take photos? I'd love to put one up in my window. Come through and make yourself at home."

I had to say 'thank you'. I really didn't want to, but I had to. After all, he had a phone.

I dialled Walt's number and waited for an answer. But there was no answer. I tried again, and then a third time but there was no answer. Walt was out. I was now in despair.

"Did you get through?" Mr. Price asked.

"Oh, I'm done thanks." I replied obscurely.

I walked back to school and rehearsed how I might break the news to the staff. After much soul-searching, I settled on the witty retort, 'he's not bloody in'. I think it would have gone down well but for one small problem that was outlined by Gillian.

"I've got seven infants who need the toilet." She informed me.

"Shit!" I replied.

"I didn't ask. But they can't hang on for ever."

Toilet requirements are contagious in young children. As soon as one child displays a desire to visit a toilet, twenty-six others develop an identical need and I was worried that once the news leaked, so to speak, we might be overwhelmed with requests to go inside. Of course, none of the children knew the full story yet. They still believed that they were being treated to an additional break time and were to be eternally grateful for this. But for the development of the inside toilet, we could have got away with it indefinitely. But historical developments in sanitation had a lot to answer for and I had a growing feeling that our period of grace was rapidly coming to an end.

"Keep them playing, Gillian. It'll be bound to take their minds off it. See if some of the staff want to set up some organised games to keep everybody busy." I suggested.

Gillian, spotting an opportunity to take charge of something, seized on the idea with terrifying enthusiasm and marched over to convince an unconvinced group of teachers to organise some games. Whether she inspired them or simply terrorised them we may never know, but within a short time there were races, leap-frog games and other delights taking place, all of which seemed to have caught the imagination of the majority of children.

Life was once again moving in the right direction. If this could maintain its momentum until the return of Walt, I would be a happy man.

But the rain clouds over the school field, and hence over my life, were darkening. There was an uneasy feeling to the breeze that had developed and was now stiffening in the air. And then the air became damp. It was clearly not going to be a short, sharp shower. It was not even going to be a downpour. No, instead we were going to be treated to an awful thick drizzle of the kind that manages to seep through the skin and saturate the bones.

"Sir, it's soaking!" an eleven year old girl complained. "Can we go back in?"

"It's only a quick shower! Don't worry, you're rustproof." I answered rather feebly.

"But it's cold and horrible."

"Hey, this is a special treat! You're getting an unexpected break time. Enjoy it."

"Mmm." She wasn't convinced. Nor should she be. The weather was turning foul and I could foresee endless complaints from parents regarding their children contracting colds, flu and other ailments due to being kept outside in miserable, damp weather. The Mad Woman's child would no doubt suffer from the Black Death and Leprosy as a result of this and she would devote her life to claiming compensation for the trouble it had caused her – but not for the trouble it had caused him, you understand. The problem was that most parents would have a right to complain. Many children would catch a chill and it would genuinely be my fault.

I could hear a vehicle on the drive. I quietly prayed that it might be Walt's yellow Jeep and sure enough, it wasn't. It was a delivery for the kitchen. Diane went over to see the driver and after much discussion, returned and demanded my attention.

"That's my frozen food!" she announced. "He can't keep it in his van and he can't come back later. So he's had to leave it on my doorstep. Well it won't stay frozen for ever, will it."

"No, Diane. I'm sure Walt won't be long. Look, it's not exactly hot out here and I think it'll be OK for half an hour or so. There's nothing else I can do."

"Half an hour? I'm drenched, I am. I don't want to be standing here for another half an hour."

"Well it might not be that long, I'm just guessing."

"I've got things to do. I'm half way through cooking… Shit! Shit and bugger!"

"Oh it's been a long time since we've had that on the menu."

"No! Shit! Oh bloody hell! Oh arse!"

"Diane, would you mind letting me in on the secret? I'd like to join in but I can't give it my best shot until I'm in character."

"My cookies are in the oven! They'll be burnt to a cinder. And I've got fish fingers frying. Everything'll be burning. Bloody hell! He'll have to be back soon or your fire drill might be a real bloody fire."

"OK, don't worry. I'm sure it'll be fine. Let's go up and have a look through the window and make sure there's no smoke developing."

We walked to the kitchen. We were absolutely drenched by this point and it was something of a relief to leave the noise of the children's complaints. The kitchen window was steamed up and both Diane and I tried hard to peer through and see what was happening.

"They're burnt to bloody bits, me cookies!" she announced. "There's smoke coming out of that oven, look."

There was indeed smoke coming from the oven. And the fryer looked no more healthy. I had no idea what to say.

"Dinner's knackered!" Diane exclaimed. "I can't serve that. It's burnt and unappetising."

I refrained from making the comment that was trying to break free from inside my head.

I left Diane to watch her cookies crumble and went back to the playground. Celia was just bending down to speak to a little boy.

"I'm wet!" he proclaimed.

"We all are, dear." Celia replied in a comforting voice.

"But I'm wet on the inside." He persisted.

"Has it soaked through your clothes?"

"No, I've peed myself. Nobody would let me go in and now I've done it. And I still need the toilet."

"Well, I don't think you do need it any more, do you!" Celia answered, rather uncomfortably.

"I do. I need to have a…"

"Oh dear me! Are you desperate?"

The little boy's eyes opened wide and his face became transfixed on a point beyond a tree in the near distance. And then suddenly his body relaxed. "Not any more." He said. "But I need some clean trousers."

The sight of Walt's yellow Jeep filled me with a new-found optimism. I had never been so happy to see Walt as I was at this moment. I bounded over to him as though he was the love of my life. "Nah then! What yer all doing out here in this weather, you'll catch your deaths. I came round that there corner and I thought this is irregular. They're not normally out at this time and specially not when it's pissing down. Aye, very irregular, I thought. I'll leave it with you." He said, when 'hello' would have sufficed.

"I'm glad you're back, Walt. We need you to let us in." I said.

"Let you in? What do you need me to let you in for. Can't you do it without me?"

"Usually, yes. But we've had a fire drill and left all the keys inside. We're locked out."

"I knew it were irregular! I said to myself, this is irregular. I knew it. Well I'll tell you this and I'll tell you now, that's a mistake you won't make again, nah then."

"Yes Walt. So can you get out of your car and let us in? We're drenched."

"Well, you will be, it's pissing it down. You shouldn't have come out wi' no keys when it were pissing it down."

"It wasn't pissing it down when we came out! It was fine."

"Why, how long have you been out here?"

"About an hour and a quarter." I grumbled. "That's why I could do with you letting us back in."

"Eee! You'll be as popular as a boil on t'arse, you will. This should live with you for years!"

"I know, so can we go in!"

"Well, we could if I had me keys, but they're inside." He announced.

"Inside?"

"Aye. Well I go for my break when everybody's here and working. When I come back, I can get in on account of somebody opening a door for me. Saves me carrying all me keys round. I've never banked on finding you've locked your bloody selves out when I come back.

I'd have never thought it possible!"

"So your keys are inside?"

"Hanging up in me room!"

"Bollocks."

I really didn't know how to face the staff. They had watched Walt's return with eagerness. They still believed that they would be warm and dry within a few minutes. And I had to tell them that this was not to be. I walked slowly back to where they were standing and felt the sensation of the ground pounding behind me. Walt was jogging to catch up with me.

"Looks like I'll have to break in!" he claimed when he caught me.

"Break in?"

"Aye. There's no option as I see it. I'll break in to a classroom and open its fire door."

Safety regulations decreed that all opening windows had to be fitted with stays. These devices stopped the window from opening wide enough for a child to jump out. Walt's first line of attack, however, was to arm himself with a screwdriver from his Jeep and prise open a top-hinged window. He would then attempt to slide in as far as possible and unscrew the stay. He explained that if this ingenious plan failed, he would put a brick through the bugger.

As he began to prise at the window frame, he attracted a small crowd of onlookers. This quickly turned into the whole school, most of whom had seen the benefits of getting a lesson in how to break in to the building as neatly as possible. Most children at this point had begun to understand the reason for our long spell of exposure to the elements and those not suffering from hypothermia were starting to see the funny side of it.

Walt prised with his long, strong tool. The edge of the aluminium frame began to bend very, very slightly. This allowed Walt to get his screwdriver in a little further and with more purchase on the proceedings he was able to force the frame a few more millimetres. He stood up to take a rest and the children listened with baited breath as Walt, the 'Poor Man's Raffles' began to utter advice to them. "It's a right bastard, this is! Nah then." were his words of wisdom. These words were duly noted by any child who wished to follow in his footsteps, but only when the wind was in the right direction.

After a moment's rest he began to work the window once more. There was now an air of anticipation as the children and staff alike watched for the tiniest movement of the frame. There were gasps as the window began to slowly inch its way from its seat. Everyone, it seemed, had momentarily forgotten that they were wet, cold and thoroughly pissed off. And with a sound like a toad farting through a microphone, the window broke free. It opened as far as its stay would allow it to go. Walt was a hero and the children cheered. His next task was to attempt to unscrew the stay so that the window would swing fully open. This entailed him standing with his back to the wall and adopting a posture similar to that which a limbo dancer might adopt. He would then attempt to slide his arms and upper torso through the bottom of the opening, thus allowing him access to the screws he so desperately needed.

Ensuring his boiler suit was securely fastened at its most crucial part, he began the process. He bent low and put his arms into the gap, allowing his head and shoulders to follow. He emitted many new and curious phrases as he followed through this procedure, most having some reference to human excrement or individuals of questionable parentage.

I was transfixed like everyone else at this point and this was something of a pity. It meant that I did not observe the car that parked on the drive and nor did I see its driver emerge. I did not notice that he walked to the main entrance and, not being able to enter the building, decided to then come to where all the action was. I didn't see him standing at the back of the crowd just as there was an excited gasp following Walt's first turn of the screw. I was too busy gasping excitedly.

The screw began to turn and Walt looked at his devoted audience and put his thumb up to them. This act was, in hindsight, a mistake. It caused his screwdriver to work loose, first from the screw head and then from his hand. It bounced off Walt's forehead, producing a cry of 'twat' as it did so, and landed on the classroom floor, prompting Walt to call out the oft-used diplomatic phrase, 'bugger, bollocks and bastard.' This was the point when Walt realised he had been steadily forcing himself deeper and deeper into the small opening made by the window. He was now rather embarrassingly stuck and required the assistance of anyone who had a blocked nose to pull him free. Four brave eleven-year-old boys came to his rescue and pulled strenuously at various parts of his anatomy until Walt emerged from his place of imprisonment, happy, but unlikely to ever procreate again.

Still unaware that I had a visitor, I joined in the cheering as Walt announced, "Well, I said there were two ways to do it. That were me tidy way, there'd have been no mess, you see. But seeing as it didn't work, I'll do it me other way. I'm going to put a bloody brick through it. Cover your eyes, we don't want an elf and safety!" And he picked up the brick – the one that he'd brought 'just in case' – and slammed it through the glass. The sound of the shattering glass was drowned out by the cheering of the children and as Walt cleared the broken glass from around the window frame I observed the children with a smile. As Walt climbed through the window to open the fire door I looked around at the faces of my pupils. And that was when I realised that there was one, additional face in the crowd.

It was the face of Tim, my LEA adviser. In fact, it was not just his face – his entire body had come along too. And he was looking with immense curiosity at the mass of drenched children, shivering with cold and learning how to effect an illegal entry to one of the Local Authority's premises.

"I've got some up-to-date figures and information for you. Thought it might be useful reading before your inspection." He said, eyeing me with curiosity.

"Thanks." I answered, blandly.

"I was just passing. I'll, er, be off then."

"OK."

"Is everything going well?" he asked, unable to contain his puzzlement.

"Of course." I replied, rather enjoying this moment of obvious intrigue.

"It's just that I couldn't help noticing…"

"Yes?"

"Well, I couldn't help noticing that everyone was outside and, well…"

"Yes?"

"Well, watching the caretaker demonstrate how to break in to the school."

"Ah, you noticed that!"

"Yes, now I know you're keen on education being relevant to the children, but…"

"Yes I am."

"Are you quite sure you can justify what was going on?"

"Absolutely. I can justify what you saw, without any difficulties at all."

"I'd be very interested to know how."

"Oh it's simple. I wanted the children to get back into the building so that they could get warm and dry. I can't see anyone arguing with that."

He clearly thought I'd gone mad. He didn't dare to ask the obvious follow-up question and I didn't have any intention of embarrassing myself by offering this information. He started towards his car and then stopped, turned and walked back to me. "How do you mean, you wanted to get the children back into the building?"

"Come inside. I'll tell you all about it."

As I explained the whole saga, Tim became almost human. He laughed and smiled in all the right places and within a short time I felt we had made more headway than in our entire official meeting before Christmas. "I would appreciate this being kept out of the public arena, Tim." I explained. "I don't want to turn up at the next Headteachers' meeting and being greeted by a bunch of clowns saying that we can't get into the building, so can I demonstrate my smash and grab skills!"

"I won't say a word." He agreed. "I can't guarantee that all your pupils will be so tactful though."

"Oh, that's a lost cause. I'm preparing myself for months of mileage over this."

Tim looked a little more serious and said, "I shouldn't really tell you this, but I've looked through your S4, the copy you sent to the LEA."

"And?"

"And it's excellent! You should've got yourself off to a cracking start with the inspection team with what you've put on that form. Just live up to it next week – and keep your keys in your pocket!"

"I intend to superglue the key ring to an intimate part of my anatomy!"

He left and wished me good luck. I presumed this was for the inspection rather than the fictitious affixing of the keys. But you never can tell with some people.

Spring Term: Week 5

In order to meet the inspection team's unobtrusive demands, I hastily rearranged my entire morning.

Inspection Week had finally arrived. It was time for the school and everyone working in it to go under a very powerful microscope. The lenses would not be rose-tinted, rather they would begin the week smeared with manure and during the course of the week it would be the job of my staff and myself to wipe them clean. Hopefully a clear view, agreeable to all of us, would emerge.

I arrived incredibly early on Monday morning, not so much as to look impressive, but more to stop the inspectors snooping through things without my knowledge. Although I could not stop them from looking in 'private places', I at least wanted to know where they had looked so that I could prepare my defence.

The teachers also arrived early, for much the same reason. Their cars were laden down at the back end by full boots of worksheets and booklets that had been photocopied from non-photocopiable books. These would remain in situ until the end of the week because the inspectors could not demand access to private vehicles. Whilst two teachers were in the toilets being sick with nerves, Nigel Blackwell, the leader of the team informed me that my office would be commandeered for the duration of the inspection and that I would have to find somewhere else to work. He then informed me that the team would be as unobtrusive as possible and we should carry on exactly as normal.

Attempting to do just that, I began to move as much of my immediate workload as I could into a corner of Ann's office. Nigel appeared once more to point out that whilst they had every desire to be unobtrusive, they would have to demand unimpeded access to the copying machine ahead of any other staff who might need it, priority access to telephone and Internet lines and their own kettle. I would also need to be available at nine o'clock to attend a preliminary discussion regarding classroom observation schedules and teacher interviews. In order to meet their unobtrusive demands, I hastily rearranged my entire morning.

I passed a message around the school to inform all the staff that the inspectors would be with me for the first half an hour and then I set off to attend the meeting. I was introduced to the entire team. There were four inspectors. Nigel was in charge and repeated this point many times over. He explained that as an ex-headteacher he knew the workings of a primary school like the back of his hand. With his incisive mind he could cut through the place like a knife through butter. I presumed that once he met some of our children, he would find our butter thicker than the average. A lady called Paula Evans was described, rather unfortunately in my view, as the next most prominent member. She had been Head of German at a secondary school on the South Coast. Quite how she was qualified to inspect a primary school in a rural, ex-mining district eluded me for the time being. Third in line was Dick Hague, a special needs teacher who was hot on hearing-impaired children. After listening to him explain this I said 'pardon' but my joke fell on deaf ears. Last and quite definitely least was the Lay Inspector. Each team has to have a member who has no background in education at all. And ours, Bridget Henelly, was eminently qualified, being unable to compose a coherent sentence and seemingly having never even been to school.

"Down to business, then!" Nigel said. "I won't beat about the bush, going round the houses isn't my style. Straight to the point, rough with the smooth, we'll talk about standards. Been looking at your Picsi and it's an interesting little chap in many ways."

A Picsi, incidentally, is no relation to Walt's elf and safety, it is a Pre Inspection Contextual data information sheet that gives the inspectors trends in pupil performance. It only gives results, however, not the reasons behind them.

"Looks to me," he continued, being unaware that the above paragraph had been inserted, "that when the children come into your school as little ones they score about average for their age. Now, when they leave you at eleven, they also score about average for their age."

I smiled and nodded. Clearly, we were ensuring the children made progress at a decent rate.

"Question!" he barked. "What are you doing in-between? Why are they still average? Strikes me there's something you're not doing. Part of the inspection will involve us looking for that little something. If you think you're already doing it, get me the evidence. Added value, that's what we're looking for in a good school. Right, whilst you ponder that, let's go over the schedules. The morning's inspections will involve Paula, Dick and myself getting into classrooms to see lessons first hand. Each teacher should, as we agreed on my last visit, leave a full lesson plan for us to look at so that we can see what's going on and where it fits in to the big picture. Bridget will stay with you and go through pupil admin. She'll inspect attendance registers, she'll look at your absence statistics and she'll see what you have in place to keep track of children who leave early or arrive late. Doctors' appointments and so on, need to know how you keep on top of who's in and out for fire regs."

We had no such book, so I offered the team a drink at his point and happily they accepted. I rushed out of the office and found Ann. "Ann, get an exercise book and fill in a list of kids' names. Put down late arrival times and early departure times for special appointments. Make it run from September. Just two or three a week to make it realistic. We're supposed to have a list for fire regulations, apparently"

"But I can't remember who went to the doctor's back in September."

"I know you can't. Make it up. Use different pens. Make it look like we've been doing it all the time. Then put it on a shelf in the office so we can look at it later."

"Ooh, isn't it exciting! Secret assignments! I feel like a spy." She giggled.

"And bring them a drink in as well."

"Oh, that's spoilt it. Spies don't make coffee!"

"So, spike it with hallucinogenics!"

Back in my office Nigel gave me a list of the lessons to be observed. Each member of the team had specialist subjects and so they would observe appropriate lessons. I intended to make a copy of this list and let the teachers see it so that they knew when to expect a visit. I wanted to make their week as comfortable as I possibly could. The schedules were complicated as they had to match individual inspectors with specific lessons on the timetable. Nigel, the unobtrusive one, wanted me to rearrange the school timetable but I refused. That would involve reorganising room and equipment usage and would leave us open to criticism if there was a mix-up. After ten minutes there was a knock at the door and Ann appeared carrying a very welcome tray.

"Your coffee, shaken, not stirred!" she announced, still evidently feeling like a spy.

"Thank you Moneypenny!" I replied and Ann giggled frantically. Bridget, the Inspector without Profiterole, looked puzzled and smiled in a way that suggested she really hadn't a clue why she was there or what was indeed happening. I hoped I could keep it that way.

By nine-forty the coffee was drunk and I wished that I were! No longer able to contain them in my office, I accepted Nigel's suggestion that we should have a brief tour of the school. If I could drag this out until the morning break, I would have saved the staff from one potential lesson observation. I stood up to lead the party on my standard tour of the school, the one I used with prospective parents. As I stepped into the corridor I was met by Ann, blocking my way and shaking her head whilst enunciating the meaningful phrase, "Mmm, mmm, mmm!"

"I'm taking the inspectors on a quick tour of the school, Ann." I told her.

"Mmm, mmm, mmm!" she replied, still shaking her head.

"Can I come past?" I asked quietly.

"Mmm, mmm!" she said, this time indicating something behind her.

There were two ways through the school. One route took us directly into a corridor from which the classrooms could be entered; the other route took us into the hall, where the journey could be taken in reverse. Assuming there was a problem in a classroom, I boldly stated, "We'll start with the hall."

"MMM, MMM!" cried Ann, now in a state of panic. I had clearly made the wrong decision.

Having been heard by the inspection team, however, there was little I could do but start with the hall. As we rounded the corner and entered the hall I could see a class of children sitting amidst an array of gymnastics equipment. They were strangely quiet and were all looking in the same direction. But for the fact that I could hear nothing, I would have assumed the teacher was talking to them. A little perplexed, I ventured further into the hall and it was at this point that I became aware of a child lying on the floor, in some considerable pain. The view of this child had up until now been hidden by a corner of a wall, but now the feet and legs were in clear view. Attempting to keep the inspectors behind me, I inched forward and Celia, the class teacher looked across in despair. As more of the child came into view it became clear that someone was attending to the boy's upper body. This particular someone was, however, wearing a green uniform and I found this unusual. Still trying to hide all this from the inspectors' view, I crept a little deeper into the hall.

This was the point at which I realised the full extent of the situation. The people in green uniforms were paramedics. They had reversed an ambulance up to the French doors in the hall and were in the final stages of fitting a neck brace to the unfortunate child. Fearing this would be difficult to hide from the inspectors I did the next best thing. I tried to ignore it.

"This is the hall." I announced, stepping over the casualty. "We use it for PE, assemblies, eating, concerts. And it has handy ambulance access for those little emergencies. I think we should move on." I led the inspectors rapidly into the first classroom. They followed me, still glancing back at the injured child and the ambulance. The first classroom belonged to Paul who, being the best-qualified first-aider in the school, was attending the disaster in the hall. Bursting into the room and not connecting this with the fact that I had just passed Paul in the hall, I announced, "Right, this is a class…without a teacher." The inspectors remained stony faced.

I led them out of the room and sighed. "It doesn't happen every day, honestly." I told them.

"It's an accident." Paula the German teacher reassured me.

"Accidents happen, and it doesn't matter how well organised you are. What matters is that the staff knew you were busy and they got it sorted out without bothering you. That's a sign of a good team if ever there was one."

I always said I had the utmost respect for that woman!

In all fairness, the rest of the tour went well. The behaviour in the school was excellent, including that of the children. By the morning break, I was feeling far less suicidal and much happier to simply mutilate myself.

With the inspectors ensconced in classrooms after the break, I attempted to indulge myself in some work. However, as is often the case, the opening of a file produced an interruption with startling immediacy. The interruption came in the form of a Local Authority van, emblazoned with the words 'Technical Support Services' on the side. The driver of the van opened the back doors and pulled out a computer. It was Ann's little smoker, returned as good as new and ready for action. I decided it might be prudent to put down my work and listen to what he had to say.

"Morning, love!" was what he had to say.

"Hello dear. Have you brought my computer back?" Ann responded, demonstrating her laser-like grasp of all things technological.

"No, I've brought you a box of chips!" the man replied with a combined snort and snigger. He was clearly proud of his play on words and was surely wasted in his role of computer repairer. He placed the machine on Ann's desk according to her instructions, plugged it in despite her plea that he shouldn't and switched it on.

"Is it better?" Ann asked.

"Well, it's better than it was! We've burnt out your hard drive but I think we've rescued quite a bit of your data, so it shouldn't be too much of a disaster."

"That'll be what made the smoke then, dear. The burning out. My driveway must have been on fire or something. Do you think so?"

"Well, I agree with the 'or something'. Let's have a look at what data we've recovered. How are you with backing up?"

"I find it hard, I think a lot of women do. I often turn the steering wheel the wrong way. But I only tend to do any backing up in the school car park. My husband drives the rest of the time."

"I mean backing up on your computer. Do you regularly back up on your computer?"

"I've never done that! That can't be what caused the problem. I never take the computer out of the office and even if I did, I'd never back over it!"

"No! I mean taking back ups of your work, copies on floppies!"

"Oh, you mean putting the disc thing in the little slot and telling it to save the work? Oh I do that, dear. You should have said that's what you meant!"

"So you do that regularly?"

"When I remember. I do it at least once every couple of months."

"Once every couple of months? Right, well, you'll need to see what's lost and what isn't when we go into the system. Hopefully, if things are lost from your hard drive, they'll be on your back ups."

"And if they aren't, will you have still got them in your office?"

The man's face contorted as he gave an incredulous look at Ann. He began entering the system and asked Ann to sit with him. "Let me know if you think anything's missing." He said.

"It looks fine to me. There's a keyboard, a screen, oh, what about the mouse mat?" she replied, impressively.

"Data!" the man grumbled. "Is there any data missing?"

"Oh I've no idea, dear. There's far too many things on there for me to know whether anything's missing. I'm glad to have it back though."

"Really?" both the man and I asked together.

"Yes. Well, there's a horrible stain on this desk and it looks such a mess. The computer covers it up perfectly. I don't like to see stains and things, do you? They're so unsightly."

The man wisely chose to ignore Ann and methodically checked through the programmes to ensure that all the LEA's systems were installed. Ann, feeling the need to demonstrate her own technological prowess, went to put the kettle on. As I looked over the man's shoulder I watched him enter the finance programme. Since hearing of Ann's reluctance to make floppy copies I was somewhat concerned that the school's current financial state might not be adequately reflected on a semi burnt out hard drive.

"Just go into a full budget report for me." I asked the man. With two hundred and twenty-six budget headings and thousands of invoices and contracts being paid, I needed to check that the information on the screen approximated to my calculations.

The man and I stared at the screen in stunned silence as the information was displayed. The technical office had re-installed the finance information, but it wasn't ours. They had put the entire Local Authority's budget on it instead. As a consequence, I apparently had a budget of several hundreds of millions, as opposed to a little over half a million. And I still had seventy-six and a half million pounds available to spend before the end of the financial year. So maybe I could replace the broken video player in the infants!

"Shit, I'll have to take it back!" was the man's response. "No, leave it! I'm very, very happy with it!" was my suggestion. "Here's your coffee." Was Ann's contribution to the proceedings as she returned.

"I'm sorry love, I've got to take it back again. We've messed up big time. I'll try and have it back to you within a couple of days. Sorry for the inconvenience."

"Oh it's alright." Ann announced, quite happily. "I've found a lovely old blotting pad in the stock room, you know, the kind that bank managers used to have on their desks. Well, that'll cover the stain up perfectly. So you can keep it as long as you like."

By the end of the day, eight teachers had been observed at least once and three had been subjected to in-depth interviews about their subject knowledge and subject leadership roles in the school. All were glad that the first day was over.

Walt was hovering around and jangling keys as he looked at the inspectors rooting through policies and work schemes. He came over to me and in a voice that felt a little too loud for comfort, said, "Are they going to piss off, then, these inspectors. I'm ready to lock up, I am."

"You go, Walt." I told him. "I'll lock up when they finish. I don't know how long they'll be, but they'll want to talk to me a lot more before we go."

"Don't they have homes to go to? I mean, you don't want to be stuck here waiting, do you. You've got your wife and kids waiting for you. They don't expect you to have a bloody life, they don't. Shall I tell 'em it's time to piss off?"

"No Walt. I know it's a pain but it goes with the job. You go home."

After the inspectors had dug through many, many files they treated me to a two-hour interview. I finally locked the doors at eight forty-five. I had no idea whether we were on course to pass or fail.

Tuesday

It was Paul's turn on the rota to take the whole school assembly. This was something of a mixed blessing as, although Paul was a wonderful story-teller and held the children in the palm of his hand for the entire twenty-five minutes, he often forgot to finish with a prayer. Now, this might sound a little unimportant and under normal circumstances it wouldn't worry me, but assemblies are official acts of collective worship. If an inspector observes an assembly without a prayer it leads to severe criticism of the school's spiritual and moral standing.

And this explains why I positioned myself at the back door of the hall where Paul could see me but the children couldn't. Ensuring the inspector was busily looking at either Paul or at the behaviour of the children I stood with my hands together, miming the word 'prayer' to Paul. I intended to stay there until I had seen a prayer take place. Clasping my hands and nodding my head furiously I became aware of a presence behind me. I turned to face Bridget Henelly, the Lay Inspector. Still with my hands clasped in prayer, I smiled at her and received no expression of response from her. Eventually, she asked, what I was doing.

"Ah, nasty case of arthritis in the shoulder. It helps if I push my hands together in that position. Takes the pain off. I'll, er, just do it a bit more to make sure it's gone." I lied.

She seemed to accept the crap that I just fed her and continued onward to her destination. I provided Paul with one more reminder and then relaxed as I saw the children begin to pray. At least we had one thing that they couldn't fail us on!

I had to call to Alma's reception class at ten-fifteen and on entering I could see a very nervous Alma talking to a group of children. In the corner there was an inspector interviewing a five-year-old boy about his work.

"It's three pigs." Said the boy. "Their mum's kicked 'em out like my mum did wi' me big sister. And there's this Big Bad Wilf and he comes and says he'll huff and puff and kick their heads in. And these pigs are scared of him."

"And what happens next?" said Paula, the inspector.

"I don't know yet. But Big Bad Wilf might get his mates round to give these pigs a good kicking."

"And what do you think the story means?" said Paula.

"I don't know." Said the boy.

"Well, why do think you've been learning the story?"

"Cos you were coming!" the boy replied, quite openly.

"And do you like the story?"

"No it's crap!"

I left, pondering how the inspectors would blame us for this child's home life that involved 'giving people a good kicking' and booting your children out of the house.

During the morning break I came across Nigel inspecting the contents of the Maths area. Blocking access to this area was a four-foot square plastic contraption containing blocks showing the numbers from one to a hundred. These were mounted, in rows of ten, on metal rods. The blocks rotated to show maths facts. Nigel, wishing to look in more detail at what equipment we provided for the children, picked up this huge square, whereupon it promptly fell to bits, scattering blocks, rods and washers all over the floor. Nigel spent the next fifteen minutes attempting to reassemble this item and did not get to see the Maths area. I later learned that Gillian had heard him say he wished to visit this area and consequently, she had loosened various parts of the number square and placed it in his way. She had rightly assumed that if he had to fix the thing back together, it might stop him snooping, at least for the time being.

A similar element of sabotage occurred in, of all places, Alan's classroom after the morning break. He was teaching his children how to plot the position of an object using the triangulation method. Discovering that he was being inspected during this session, he decided the object to be triangulated would be Paul, the inspector. Thus, thirty-two children came at the inspector from various angles, each holding a tape measure. They triangulated the inspector from various corners of the room and plotted his position accurately on a plan. This had the advantage of preventing the inspector from walking around the room and also, from leaving it. By the end of the lesson he had been unable to fill in any of his observation notes but at least he was aware of his precise location in the classroom. Sabotage and conspiracy were clearly things that Alan did well!

The afternoon began with a wonderfully ironic event. Bridget, the Lay Inspector, had been nibbling on a fingernail – fortunately it was one of her own – for around a quarter of an hour, when it began to bleed profusely. She had used this moment as an excuse to ask a child where the first-aid box might be found and was impressed that the child could answer this question accurately. The box was attached to a wall in Ann's office and Bridget resolved to obtain a plaster for her finger. She opened the door to the box, took out a pack of plasters and began attaching one to her appendage. There was, at this point, a loud groaning sound and the first-aid box, as if aware that it were in the vicinity of an inspector, fell off the wall. It landed squarely on Bridget's arm, bruising it badly. I had to admit to a certain degree of amusement when I learned that she had been injured by a falling first-aid box but I did my duty and checked immediately that nothing was broken. The box was indeed intact and so I left Walt in charge of refitting it.

Much of my afternoon was to be spent discussing the school's finances with the aforementioned Bridget. We pulled out the most recent budget reports and backed these up with the minutes of the Governors' Finance Committee. This committee had the job of assisting me in making informed decisions regarding the allocation and monitoring of the school's budget. In reality, the members knew zilch about accounting and budget control and so they simply agreed to everything I suggested. In some respects this is fine, but in other ways it allows the Head too much power and in my case, was accompanied by a feeling of uneasiness.

Bridget was unhappy with how much of the budget had been spent. At this point in the year, early February, there were around seven weeks left in the current financial year. Only twenty-four thousand pounds were left and I expected to overspend by six thousand.

"I want you to explain why you will overspend." She began. "You're supposed to be running like a business and a business wouldn't blandly overspend. It would cut back. It comes down to good financial planning at the outset."

"My financial planning was very clear." I explained. "The reason I will overspend is because the Government tend to decide, mid-way through a year, that we should carry out a particular initiative and that this will require us to employ a set number of hours of non-teaching help. When I question where the money will come from, I'm told 'it has to come out of your budget'. I don't get a choice whether to do it or not – it's Government policy so I have to do it. But this comes *after* I've committed the rest of the budget. How many businesses operate under those circumstances? How many would survive if they did? My financial planning means nothing if the Government keeps changing the rules as the year progresses."

"Have you never heard of a contingency? You need to put money aside for such situations."

"When the budget only just covers the running costs, it's difficult to set aside a useful contingency. My staff costs take up ninety-one percent of my budget and yet my classes are still too big – I don't have enough teachers. Buildings related costs and fuel bills take up another five and a half percent. Buying into LEA services takes up three percent and that leaves me with three thousand pounds to spend on actually educating children. And you want me to set a contingency aside?"

"Well a school of your size should have a much healthier balance at this point in the year." She insisted. "The average budget for a school of this size is seven hundred and eighty thousand pounds. You appear to have spent seven hundred and fifty-six thousand of it."

"My school is in a poorly funded authority. My budget this year is six hundred and one thousand. I have actually spent five hundred and seventy-seven thousand."

"I'm sorry, I can only work on average figures."

"Then what do I do to squeeze nearly another two hundred grand from the LEA?"

"My job is to inspect, not to advise."

"Right, well go and inspect this. In certain local authorities, each child is worth an extra six hundred pounds in the school budget than they are around here. That's an extra one hundred and eighty thousand pounds for a school with three hundred pupils. That money goes directly to providing extra teachers, extra equipment, decent working conditions like roofs that don't leak, and so on. In other words, the kids get a better education system. In our area we dig ourselves into holes trying to balance budgets that are impossibly tight. We can't buy in sufficient staff, we can't have the suggested number of computers. We make ourselves ill worrying about overspending and yet in many counties, my overspend of six thousand would translate into an *underspend* of well over a hundred and fifty thousand. I could build a whole new computer suite with that! Here's my actual budget figures – work on these before you criticise!" I slapped a sheet in front of her face and walked out of the room. Half an hour later, to her credit, she had looked at the numbers and made a momentous decision. Heads in our part of the world were working wonders on pathetically small budgets and the whole system was very unfair. She chose to say in her report that financial planning was excellent and decided to look no further into the matter. This was good, as I didn't want her to get wind of Gillian's raffles!

Her next item for inspection was Health and Safety. After spending time with me in reading our terrifyingly detailed Health and Safety Policy, she needed to see how it was put into practice. For this, I handed her over, at her request, to Walt. He would be the man to walk her through the system and I apprehended him on the corridor near the staff room.

"Walt!" I called. "This is Bridget. She's got an interest in Health and Safety. Can you take her for a walk round school and show her how we take care of things?"

"If I must. Only I'll tell you this and I'll tell you now and I'll tell you reight and straight and when it's said it's said, I'll need to be done in half an hour. Sanitation waits for no bugger. What's your name then, duck?"

"Bridget." She replied, quite sure of her argument.

"And what do you do?"

"I'm a lay inspector." She informed him.

"Nah then, there's a thing. It's surprising what gets inspected these days. So when you say 'lay inspector', are we talking about chickens or shagging! You should have been here when we had travellers up at our pond. That'd have given you plenty to inspect!"

"Oh, er, oh, oh! I inspect things in schools that have nothing to do with education." She attempted to explain.

"Well, you're in t'right place. This school doesn't have much to do with education. I'll leave it with you!"

"No, no. I inspect the non-academic parts of a school. I'm not qualified in educational matters, you see."

"Oh! Sounds like a doddle of a job. How'd you swing a cushy number like that then? Do you have to know t'boss man? Is that why you're called a lay inspector? Anyway, I can't stand here talking all day. If you want to see some elf and safety you'd better come wi' me. I'll show you my urinals."

With a feeling of satisfaction, I watched as Bridget and Walt walked off, if not into the sunset, at least into the toilet. She would receive a treat equal to nothing she had ever before experienced.

Some time later I chanced upon the two of them still partaking in the tour. Bridget had not only inspected the urinals but had been granted access to Walt's assortment of nuts and had been shown the most effective way to handle a scrubber. During this informative session, Joan the cleaner blew in for her shift. Worried at first that Walt might be lavishing attention on another, she gave Bridget a chilly reception, but once the finer points of the social gathering had been explained, Joan gave a loud, contented belch and offered to show Bridget the warping window sill in the Year Four classroom as a gesture of friendship.

Although I was unable to get away until ten-fifteen, it had been a mildly successful day. And we were halfway through the inspection.

Thursday

By the morning of our final day of inspection I was still unclear about the direction it was taking. Some things had gone well but others were more questionable. Most of the lessons observed had been at least satisfactory but I was left with a niggling feeling that every positive statement would be qualified by a 'but'. I wanted to joke that every statement would be qualified by a Big Butt when I remembered that Nigel would be writing the final report, but joking was not appropriate at this stage.

The previous night the team had given me a list of school qualities for which they had found no evidence. Today was the day we had to provide such evidence or accept that the report would not give favourable references for those aspects. Some were a little difficult – parts of the Sex Education programme that was planned for July, drama classes which were not on the timetable for this term, and so on – but other evidence would be found and rammed under the inspectors' noses.

We would have until early afternoon to complete this. After that, the inspectors would take me into 'their' office and tell me, over the course of around five hours, about what they intended to include in the report. This would be a happy time for the staff, as there would be a guarantee of no lesson observations but it would be an intense time for me, as I would have to try to argue my case for anything I wasn't happy with in the report.

Nigel came for a chat late in the morning. He explained that whilst the school was what he would term 'basically OK', he had some concerns about our local area. Our test results could be higher if the children had more support at home. Some of the children's behaviour could be better they had more discipline at home. He seemed to be telling me that we were doing a decent job against, if not all, some of the odds. But then came the bombshell. "So you need to look at how you can improve the background support for your children. Have you thought about holding workshops for parents? Have you considered 'good parenting classes'? Have you tried to get parents in at weekends and evenings to make them aware of what goes on in school? With a bit of imagination you can run a whole range of courses to help your mums and dads become more effective parents. That will have a beneficial effect on the children."

I had a problem with this. "At the risk of sounding selfish, Nigel, I'm not sure I want to run evening and weekend classes for parents. We're a school, we educate children. I don't see why we have to take responsibility for the whole of society."

"It benefits your kids." He replied glibly.

"And what about my staff? And what about me? When do we spend time with our families? When do I become a supportive parent to my children if I'm spending every waking minute sorting out everyone else's family?"

"It's part of the job. You have to expect it."

"No, I work long hours already. I take endless piles of work home every night. If I start suggesting parent classes, my staff won't agree to do it. Remember, they don't get overtime pay – it's all part of a single salary and they're not going to give up evenings and weekends for nothing. And that means I'll have to do it myself and I'm sorry, but I need a life too!"

"Not looking good, then. I'll have to note that these measures were suggested but that the school declined to take an interest. Not a nice thing to have in your report."

"I don't think you can do that!" I snapped.

"Well, you can complain, but there's a time delay. The report will be published by the time anything gets discussed."

This worried me. The man had a bee in his bonnet about parenting classes and I was expected to fall into line because of his whim. I didn't disagree with the idea, I just didn't want to take on even more work. It would put pressure on my family life and there would be inevitable problems when something happened that displeased someone. And all this for no pay? I was happy to allow the school to be used by qualified instructors but that wasn't an option. This was to be done on the cheap, by staff who felt backed into a corner. I moaned about it to other staff over lunch and they all agreed with me.

At two o'clock I was summoned to see the inspectors. I sat, facing the four of them, as they held hastily produced draft copies of the report. They read, expressionless, for the entire period. I listened to each paragraph and either agreed or asked if a statement could be qualified a little better. To my surprise, Nigel was surprisingly amenable to my suggestions and assumed that he was doing this in readiness for his piece de resistance, the parenting classes.

But this was still not to be. He made a few statements about children's progress being partly dependent upon different levels of support at home but this was said in a way which was derogatory to neither the parents nor the school. I was pleasantly surprised and, whilst puzzled, I remained determined to not ask why he had changed his mind so quickly.

By seven o'clock we were ready to leave. The report was going to show us as a good school, staffed by caring people who had the children's best interests at heart. Judging by the pitiful budget available to us, we offered good value for money, apparently. We had been 'awarded' three basic criticisms, all of which were things we could do nothing about due to having a crap budget. However, in true Ofsted fashion, I had to produce a very, *very* detailed action plan to show how these criticisms would be addressed before the next inspection. I had forty days in which to produce the plan, get my governors to approve it and then send it to Ofsted. Bearing in mind that my governors would approve the ingredients of a box of corn flakes if I presented them as an action plan, I had no fears that they might argue over the finer points of the wording.

At home, just on the verge of taking my family out for a meal to remind them of who I was, the telephone rang. Not wanting to become embroiled in school business any further, I left the answer machine to pick up the call, but was surprised when the voice on the other end belonged to Paul, the Year Four teacher. He was never the kind of person to ring with problems in the evening and so I rushed to the phone and picked it up.

"Did the final meeting go well?" he asked.

"Very well, actually. They even changed their tune over the weekend and evening classes. There's no mention of it. I'm a bit surprised, to tell you the truth."

"I think I know why." Said Paul. "I read on Nigel Blackwell's CV that he used to be a headteacher in Rotherham. Well, a friend of mine, a guy I went to university with, started teaching in Rotherham and stayed there because he thought it was a good LEA to work for. I gave him a ring to ask if he'd ever heard of Nigel Blackwell and he nearly fell off his chair! It turns out that Nigel used to be the head of my mate's school. My mate worked for him for five years. The guy was an abysmal headteacher. He buggered up the school budget so badly that the LEA had to get involved to bail the place out – after three teachers had been made redundant – and his overall grip on the school was non-existent. The behaviour of the kids dropped to an all-time low, relationships with parents were appalling and not one of the staff had any respect for the man. And then he heard his school was due for an inspection, back in the days when you got six months' notice. So what did he do? He got a secondment and went off to train to be an Ofsted inspector. Seems he couldn't run his own school properly so he decided to go and criticise other people running theirs! Oh, and his school failed its inspection due to having had an extended period of poor leadership and management. But he'd gone by then!"

"Fantastic work, Paul! So what did you say to him?"

"Not much. I just casually mentioned that I'd happened to bump into Richard Edwards and, what a coincidence, 'he worked at your school, didn't he Nigel'! After that he changed colour slightly, made an excuse and left. I had a feeling he wouldn't make waves."

"You're a star, Paul! I'm going to find a way to pay you back for this!"

"Tell you what, let me have whatever's left in the budget at the end of the year!" he joked.

"OK, you owe me six grand!"

The meal with my family was doubly delicious.

Spring Term: Week 6

"Not what you expect from a safety event. Whole bloody class ending up visiting hospital doesn't fit in with the spirit."

After an inspection, schools fall into a lull. The adrenaline has been sapped away and nobody wants to particularly do anything. We had two more weeks before half term and I was happy to let people drift aimlessly toward that very welcome break. I intended to drift even more aimlessly and would clearly be unaware of what was going on anyway!

However, Wednesday was set to include a highly entertaining afternoon. It was the annual Safety Event for Year Six pupils and I was going to attend, along with Alan and his class. The Safety Event was a wonderful idea, to which schools were invited individually. An old warehouse and its surrounding land had been converted into a sort of educational theme park consisting of hazardous situations which the children had to tackle. Such situations taught the children how to avoid being ploughed down by a speeding truck, where best to kick an approaching pervert, how to not spark off an inferno in the bathroom, and so on. The scenarios were realistic and members of staff were employed as actors to give the session a genuine sense of reality.

Alan, his class and I walked, on this damp afternoon, to the end of the school drive, whereupon a coach would collect us and drive us the six miles to the Safety Centre. Ten minutes after our allotted pick-up time, I searched fruitlessly for any sign of a coach. The road remained quiet, the children remained loud and the dampness became damper.

"Not good enough!" Alan postulated. "Arrival time clearly stated on the letter. No sign of a bus. I'm not a lover of tardiness, never have been. Leads to unexpected surprises."

"They're the worst!" I joked. "I don't mind expected surprises, but unexpected surprises, well…"

"Bad grammar, apologies. Still, message is the same. Serious lack of bus, late arrival at centre, potentially craps up the afternoon. I'm not a lover of crapped up afternoons. Punctuality, that's the key. I'm a lover of punctuality. It's something I always strive for. Always have done!"

I found this comment interesting, bearing in mind that Alan seemed to have left it so very late to turn into a normal human being.

It rained. We began to get very wet and Alan continued moaning. In desperation I plunged my hand in my pocket and extracted my mobile phone. I rang Ann in the office and asked her to find me the number of the coach operator. She did this with fearsome speed and I dialled the number with which she had provided me. The person at the end of the line informed me that the local Bedwetting Support Group didn't provide buses to safety events and politely suggested that I may have the wrong number. On my second call to Ann, she informed me that she may have made a mistake earlier but 'bedwetting' and 'buses' were on the same page of her notepad and so it was an entirely excusable error.

Eventually I made contact with Barry's Coaches and was promised immediate redress. The manager would, he informed me, personally ring the driver and bollock him. He proceeded to inform me that this wasn't the first complaint they had had and that the driver was a lazy twat but somewhat prone to violence when riled. I thanked the man for both his help and his psychological insight, ended the call and instantly spotted the coach trickling down the hill towards our wet and waiting group. As the children boarded, I heard the driver's phone ring.

Quickly rushing the children onto the bus I made as much noise as possible to drown out the foul language issuing from the driver as he discussed time-keeping with his boss. Once the children were seated we accelerated rapidly and the driver turned to look at me. He looked in my direction for an uncomfortable length of time, considering we were travelling at forty miles per hour. "Some bastard back at your school's been complaining about me being late. It'll be yer bleeding headteacher. It's a good job he's not here! I'm just in the mood for a scrap."

I smiled and decided to talk to Alan. Alan was holding himself in an uncomfortable position, being not terribly impressed by the standard of driving on today's journey. Being Alan, he finally stood up, leaned over to the driver and tapped him on the shoulder.

"Quick word, if you don't mind!" he said. "On our way to a safety event. Like to get there alive! Looks bad having an accident on the way to a safety event."

"What yer on about?" the driver questioned.

"Think you're a bit close to the vehicle in front. Too close to stop."

"Well he'd better keep going then, hadn't he!"

"No, I'm not a lover of dangerous driving. Slippery slope, ends in disaster. Can't condone it. Lives of children in your hands, lacking responsibility. I'm a lover of responsibility, it's a thing I do well."

"There's a toilet at the back of this bus. If yer going to chuck out any more crap, go and do it in there!"

"I'm simply asking you to…"

Alan broke off his sentence because he had other matters to attend to. The driver, as predicted, had to brake sharply. Alan, holding onto a pole just behind the driver's seat had lurched forward and head butted the pole on deceleration. His glasses had attempted to wrap themselves around the pole but had only succeeded in bending quite 'spectacularly' at their centre. Alan picked up his spectacles, straightened them and sat down. He produced a note pad, possibly from inside his beard, upon which he intended to jot down details of the incident, but as he began to write, both his lenses fell out and landed on his knee.

"Not happy." He said. "I'll make an official complaint. I'm quite proficient at complaining. It's a thing I do well. Got a bit of a headache. Do it later, I think. Got any paracetamol?"

We arrived unharmed at the safety event and we were ushered into a room without windows. A lady wearing a badge called Delia greeted us. Coincidentally, not only the badge but also the lady turned out to be called Delia. She spoke to the children in a manner which might be adopted for a pet dog or a three-year-old toddler. "Hello children." She began. "Today you will be doing some very exciting things. You will learn how to cope in dangerous situations. Don't worry, none of our situations are really dangerous because they're all carefully controlled. We don't want you going home with bumps and bruises." Why not, I wondered! They went home like that from school most nights. She continued her spiel, "Malcolm, our guide will take you round each room. You will see hazards and dangers and Malcolm will ask you questions about them. You might even have to give a description of a naughty man or lady to the police. Isn't it all exciting!" The children smiled sympathetically at Delia and set off to follow Malcolm to the first scenario.

The first room was an unpretentious little place littered with syringes, aerosol cans and foil. On the wall was a badly painted playground scene. To our great surprise, the theme here was drugs.

A man talked incessantly at the children for fifteen minutes and I could only assume that he was trying to demonstrate the mind-numbing effect that a drug might have on a young person's brain. Each child was given a plastic bag containing a pencil, a pencil sharpener and a rubber. The pencil carried the phrase 'Don't Do Drugs' on the side of it and the plastic bag contained no holes and would therefore be a danger to a small child. The children were given a quiz to complete and as I watched them work, I noticed how a number of pencils had weak leads and needed to be sharpened regularly. By the end of the session, eight children had sharpened their pencils to such an extent that the message printed on them now read 'Do Drugs'. I was impressed by the forethought of the design of a pencil that could simultaneously appeal to both extremes.

The road safety area passed without major incident and we were whisked to our next port of call. Here, a lady sat and talked about personal safety on the streets. As she did so, a middle aged, frail woman walked in behind her, hovered in the background for a while and then quietly and swiftly stole the speaker's handbag. This, it said in the teachers' notes, was to be an exercise in reporting a robbery and giving a description to the police. However, three gallant young men in our group had watched the event unfold and had chosen to take it upon themselves to apprehend the criminal, whom they believed to be genuine. As she left the room, the three boys leapt to their feet and ran towards the door. With a spectacular flying tackle they brought the frail woman to the ground and retrieved the handbag in one fell swoop. And whilst one lady received her bag, the other received three fractured ribs and had to be rushed to hospital. Personal safety on the streets was not a major issue for these children, I suspected. We moved on quickly.

By far the most impressive part of the visit was the 'fire room'. The children were informed by the custodian of this room that they would need to look for dangers that might cause a fire. They were not told that a simulated fire would then break out and they would need to exit safely through the cosmetic smoke. I knew of this because I had read my notes. Alan, conversely, had accidentally dropped his notes in a puddle shortly after arriving. He claimed to not need them as only the fire room was new since his last visit.

The children were told that in the event of a fire they should check to see if a door was hot before opening it in case the fire was behind it. They were told to lay low under the smoke so that they could breathe if difficult conditions persisted. And they were told not to panic. They entered the room and began looking for dangers. They spotted overloaded sockets, a coloured scarf draped over a lamp to give a nice pink glow, a drink precariously balanced on top of a TV, and many more subtle hazards. I was very impressed and so was the group leader. And then, just discernible in the corner of the room, smoke appeared from under the door. The children near the back of the group smelled it first. One of them coughed and then put up his hand and said, "I can see some smoke here."

"Where do you mean?" asked the leader.

"Coming from under this door." Said the boy.

Many of the children looked a little startled but tried to remember what they had been told earlier. Only one person from the entire group made a fool of himself and began to panic. It was Alan.

"Oh my God! That's real smoke! We're on fire! What are we going to do? Where's the alarm? I'm not a lover of fires. I'm not a lover of any emergencies if the truth be told."

Close to the door, a child touched the panel with the back of her hand and shouted, "It's not hot." She opened the door and a cloud of dense, dark grey smoke filled the room. In the quietness I could hear two distinct sounds. One was the movement of the children as they got down to the floor and started crawling out of the room. The other was Alan, now in a state of terror. "This is a disaster. Help! I'm not good with disasters. Keeping my head is not a thing I do well in an emergency. Somebody ring an alarm. I'm asthmatic! I can't breathe in this! Tending to panic! Help me!"

Alan, now spluttering, was the only one left in the room. The children and I had crawled out along the corridor and were looking in through the fake mirror as the cosmetic smoke was being switched off. The smoke cleared rapidly as a powerful air conditioner was put into action. And as the smoke faded away, there was Alan, coughing and shouting for help on the premise that he had a large group of children in the room and was worried about their safety. As the last of the smoke departed through the extraction vents, Alan, sweating profusely, finally noticed that he was alone. Not aware that we could see through the mirror, he looked round and finally spoke. "Well bugger me." He said, much to the children's delight. "It was all a bit of technological trickery." And then he marched out of the room and found us in the corridor.

"Are you OK?" I asked.

"Me? Fine. Just checking that no children were left in there, you know. It's surprising how they panic sometimes. Thought I'd better be sure I was the last one out. Damn clever, that smoke effect. Almost realistic!"

"Yes Alan. Almost!"

The afternoon passed very quickly and we walked outside to board the coach. This time it was waiting for us and once on board, we set off straight away. I had to admit that Alan was right about the driver. He didn't inspire confidence in his passengers and I had misgivings about his ability to take responsibility for so many lives. He drove too fast and too close. He reacted at the very last minute to changes on the road and I felt he was not especially observant. But I consoled myself with the knowledge that it was a short journey and on mainly quiet roads.

It was when the driver began opening a packet of sweets that I started to feel that things were not going to improve at all. He fiddled incessantly with the packet and the individually wrapped sweets inside. They clearly held far more importance to him than the mere task of piloting a large coach through the countryside. And then I watched as he dropped an orange flavoured chewy sweet on the floor of his cab. This obviously disappointed him, as was demonstrated by the comment 'shit, they're my favourite' and so he proceeded to bend down and fish around with his right hand in the hope that he might chance upon the dropped delicacy. He was successful in his mission. He grasped the sweet but in doing so he had inadvertently steered the coach into the centre of the road. The oncoming car found a certain degree of fault with this action and began to sound its horn and flash its lights frantically. The driver uttered what I believed to be a cry of 'bollocks', unless he was admiring young cattle in a nearby field, and swerved sharply to the left. Still clutching his orange flavoured chewy sweet he bounced the coach through a wooden fence and some considerable distance along an incredibly bumpy field before coming to rest against a tree stump.

The sound of frightened children filled the air. I stood up and looked at their terrified faces, at the coats and bags littering the centre aisle of the coach and at the trail we had left behind us, visible through the back window. We were never in any real danger because the ground was flat and there were no major obstacles that we could have hit, but we were badly shaken. Some of the children had cuts to their faces, sustained as we bounced through the ruts in the field. One boy had fallen out of his seat and onto the floor, courtesy of a faulty seat belt that had come adrift at the exact moment it was needed.

The front door was jammed where the bodywork had been bent against the tree stump. I went to the back of the coach and opened the rear exit. I tested the ground outside. It was wet and muddy but there were no holes or nasty surprises. One by one the children climbed out of the coach and stood, shivering with a combination of cold and shock, in the field. In no time at all the sound of sirens could be heard. The driver of the car had witnessed the entire event and had called the emergency services.

As the emergency vehicles arrived, the driver emerged from the coach. "Listen mate!" he said. "You will back me up, won't you? I mean, it was an accident all this. I don't need no police trouble. And I'm sure that car was going too fast for these roads. Besides, there's no real harm done."

I smiled at him and said, "I would never dream of landing anybody in it with the police."

"Cheers, pal!" he said.

"And that's why I've got no intention of blaming the man driving sedately towards us whilst you were bending down looking for a sweet."

"Aw, come on. We're not exactly dying, are we!"

"This bit of road was in your favour. In another set of circumstances you could have killed us."

"Bastard!" he concluded.

"Caring bastard, if you don't mind!" I suggested.

Alan wandered across to me as we watched the ambulance staff check the children over. He smoothed his beard as he spoke. It had clearly been a casualty of the accident. "Not what you expect from a safety event. Whole bloody class ending up visiting hospital doesn't fit in with the spirit. Never been a good passenger, it's not a thing I do well. Now I know why!"

It took three hours to make sure every child was home from the safety event in one piece. Nobody was seriously injured. Some children suffered cuts and bruises, but the only things broken were the pencils they had been given. Alan's beard was in need of a trim, but then I'd never seen it any other way so I wasn't overly concerned that he would need time off work.

As for the coach driver, he was charged with careless driving. Whilst this probably amounted to only ten minutes in jail, he did lose his job with Barry's Coaches. Apparently, Barry's empire consisted of only one coach and since that had assumed a revised shape upon hitting the substantial tree stump it was out of action for some considerable time. The detrimental effect on Barry's business was severe and the cheery driver became the first casualty of the fallen dynasty.

And three days later, several parents received a letter from a local solicitor, offering to help them sue the school for negligence. Well, at least it would save me from getting bored.

"When I were younger," the Mayor said, "we didn't have all these greenhouse gases, in fact we had to make do with an allotment in most cases, and we didn't know about the ozone because it wasn't there then."

Gillian arrived immensely excited on Thursday morning. The Mayor would be visiting and Gillian was a sucker for officialdom. She grovelled and scraped to anyone whom she felt to be in any form of influential position and it could be quite nauseating to observe if it happened without adequate warning. She extended this behaviour to councillors, parents who held powerful jobs, leaders of certain committees in the local area, but absolutely not to me! The Mayor, however, was the pinnacle of power in Gillian's eyes and his visit would result in some serious fawning.

The reason for his visit was actually quite an impressive one. As part of Gillian's role in school, she had set up committees of children to look after all things environmental. They monitored energy usage, recycled paper and lobbied the council on environmental issues. In theory, this was excellent, but some teachers had complained of being plunged into darkness whilst working in their classrooms on a darkish winter lunch break, when an 'energy monitor' burst in and switched the lights off. There was also the matter of the prize for the class that recycled the most paper, as this resulted in some children purposely wasting sheets of A4 so that they could fill the recycling box more quickly. But on the whole, the work was impressive and we had won a prestigious award for Environmental Awareness. We were to be presented with a certificate, a plaque and, of all things, a flag. This latter item would entail the erection of a flagpole, after obtaining planning permission. Walt could already see problems inherent in the erection of a flagpole and the subsequent elf and safety matters regarding the non-stranglisation of children on the ropes. "It's not just your erection!" he had informed me, "It's what you do with it afterwards to make sure nobody gets injured. I mean, you'll have kids flocking round a thing like that and if some bloody pancake tries to climb up it you could end up with an 'ospital case. And then you've got bits that dangle lower down and they can be just as tempting. We'll have to look into how they can be secured. They want trussing off." I knew exactly what he meant, and I had to agree that nobody wanted a pancake on top of their flagpole, but somehow I still felt uneasy discussing the matter in public.

So excited was Gillian that she had arranged for a classroom assistant to take charge of her class so that she could prepare for the mayoral visit. The plan was to bring the entire school into the hall for an assembly, the main focus of which would be the Mayor's speech and the presentation of the award. Gillian wanted to greet the Mayor, offer him a drink and lick the soles of his feet before he met the children.

Trying to evade continued discussion with Walt, I apprehended Gillian as she walked past me and said, "At the risk of sounding a bit thick, who is the Mayor?" I figured I should know his name if I had to introduce him.

"Jack Jarvis." Gillian replied. "His Worship, Councillor Jack Jarvis."

Walt spluttered and laughed. "Jack Jarvis? Is he about my age?"

"I imagine he is." Gillian answered.

"Jack bloody Jarvis! He lived next door but one to me when we were kids. I went to school wi' Jack Jarvis."

"Really? It'll be nice to meet him again after all this time." Gillian suggested.

"It bloody won't! I've never known such a tosser! He were the biggest bully in our school, were Jack Jarvis. And he were as thick as cow shit."

"Well, he must have changed somewhere along the line. He's the Mayor now."

"He won't have changed. He's Mayor because of two things. He's a gobby bastard and he'll have bullied his way into t'job. I shall look forward to seeing him. When's he coming?"

"Now don't go causing trouble, Walt. He'll be here any minute and I want this to be a dignified occasion."

"Dignified? Jack Jarvis dignified? I'll tell you this and I'll tell you now and I'll tell you reight and straight and when it's said it's said and I'll say no more, he's as dignified as a…, as a…, well he's bloody not dignified. I'm surprised he's not been locked up. I'd watch him wi' them kids if I were you. I wouldn't trust him as far as I could…"

Walt stopped talking because we caught sight of the black limousine parking outside the door. I vaguely recognised the Mayor from his previous visit on the occasion that he came here to present a picnic area to a school across town. His wife emerged from the car, followed by the notorious Jack Jarvis, both nodding pompously at the chauffeur as he held the door.

Gillian surged forward and slurped words of welcome at the two dignitaries. Walt stood next to me and whispered, "That's Mary Morton. She were the biggest slag our school had ever seen. She were looser than an elephant wi' diarrhoea, she were. I'd keep her away from that bloody flagpole if my memory's got anything to do with it. She'd think it were her bloody birthday. Mind you, with her on top it'd stop any bloody kids climbing up it!"

I had often wondered why Walt had never joined the Diplomatic Corps and today's descriptions of our honoured guests helped me form an opinion on that.

As His Worship was led toward the entrance, Walt gave a shout. "Nah then Jack! I always knew you'd end up wearing a chain. Trouble is, I expected it to have a ball attached to it."

"Is that Wally Balderson? Wally, how are you?"

"I'll tell you this and I'll tell you now and I'll tell you reight and straight and when it's said it's said and I'll say no more, I'm not a Wally nowadays. I'm Walt."

"Eee, Walt!" Mary announced. "Do you remember me?"

"Course I do! I only stopped having t'nighmares six months ago! Mary Morton the Man Muncher! I remember when you tried to rip me trousers off behind t'bike sheds. I never knew lasses were that strong and it put me off 'em for years."

"I'll do it again if you ask me nicely!"

"You bloody won't and I'll tell you for why. We haven't got no bloody bike sheds."

"Ooh, that won't worry me!" she said enticingly.

"You've not bloody changed, have you! Well, you're fatter and older but you know what I mean, you're still a slapper." Walt observed incisively. Yes, such a loss to the world of diplomacy.

Gillian was apoplectic. Her distinguished guests were being socially mugged by Walt. She had intended this moment to be so special, so dignified, so Walt-free, and it was all going badly wrong. She attempted in vain to break up the reunion.

"Anyway, I see you've done well for yourself!" Jack Jarvis sneered. "It must be a lovely job cleaning all these bogs every night and wiping sick up. I regret never doing it myself." He stroked his chain of office as he spoke and Walt's heckles rose as he prepared for the kill.

"Cleaning bogs? Cleaning bogs? Is that what you think I do? Let me tell you this, I have the best urinals in the Northern Hemiscope. I'm proud of my urinals. People tell me they've never seen ceramics in such good condition. And I've got waste pipes that some people would kill for. And that's before I tell you about me nuts. I could spend hours showing you what I do with me nuts and you'd still not understand me system. But if somebody wants a bit of screwing doing, I can pull out my kit in seconds on account of I know where it all is. Aye, you'll never catch me without me equipment ready. I'll leave it with you."

"We must go in!" Gillian snapped. "The children are coming into the hall and I haven't had time to brief you." And with that she took hold of the Mayor's arm and dragged him into the hall, having been unable to offer the dignified drink.

As the children assembled the Mayor began to look nervous. He didn't like talking to children, he explained. They were not a good audience. Whereas adults would generally be polite and do their best to make a speaker feel at ease, children would do the exact opposite. They would fiddle with things and if you looked at them you would lose your train of thought. If they thought you were boring, they would yawn in a very obvious way, or simply start chatting to somebody. Yes, children were a difficult audience, in his experience. I resolved to not mention that, in my experience, councillors tend to be so bloody boring that they shouldn't be surprised that nobody wants to listen.

I introduced the Mayor to the children but omitted to introduce all of the children to the Mayor. He stood up, cleared his throat and took a deep breath. He then began to speak in a monotone. "Good morning. I have been invited to your school in order to make a presentation vis-à-vis the sterling work enacted by your select committee for environmental matters. We in the council set great store by youngsters such as yourselves involving themselves in social issues such as the aforementioned. The future of our planet is heavily dependent upon the actions of people like yourselves in your attempt to make headway vis-à-vis the sustainable future of the Earth."

I looked at the faces of the children. The younger ones, those aged between four and seven, had no idea what the man was talking about. They had progressed to staring at the ceiling and counting the tiles. They longed for another visit from the window cleaner so that they might be able to watch his squeegee slide back and forth. The older children understood most of the words but were on the point of realising that the Mayor was simply repeating himself and, in actual fact, didn't really understand anything about what the children had done. This was a valuable lesson for the future, Bullshit for Beginners.

He continued droning. "When I was younger, people didn't know about the environment and so we didn't attempt to save it. In fact, I didn't even know we had one. It's like smoking, nobody knew it could kill you, some adverts said it was good for you and we believed them. Things were different then. We didn't have all these greenhouse gases, in fact we had to make do with an allotment in most cases, and we didn't know about the ozone because it wasn't there then. That's why I'm so proud of you. And when I look at your faces and think what your world will be like when you're my age, it makes me think what your world will be like when you're older. You see, we didn't have drugs, there were no joyriders and you didn't have to take a condom with you everywhere you went. It was a different world. And me and my councillor associates, we miss all that and that's why I'm so proud of you. It's like food, you see.

When we were young, my wife, that lady over there, and I, they didn't spray chemicals on your food. They didn't have these genetic foods that come from a sheep's clone with three ears. It were good and wholesome. And that's what makes me proud of you. You've done a good job in what you've done, you've recycled the ozone and you've created more electricity. Because that's what turning off lights does, you know, it creates more electricity. And if you switch your lights off, you'll make enough electricity to light up a house for two days. And you're doing it and that's why I'm so proud. And that's why you've won a flag. And I would like to present this flag and these other bits and pieces like this sistificate and a plague to put your wall on behalf of my members."

Gillian leapt up and went to the front. "Thank you, Your Worship. I'm sure the children listened carefully to what you had to say and I think the older ones will remember it for a long time." "Well, I hope so. I hope my few words will strike a chord and encourage them to make more electricity and recycle more ozone and maybe win another flag. You see, when I were their age none of this happened. We didn't have an environment and we never did these initial-tives like what you do nowadays. They've worked very hard have these youngsters and that's why I'm very proud. Well done young 'uns."

Gillian asked the Mayor to help her unfold the flag so that the children could look at it. It was indeed a huge thing and as Jack Jarvis unfurled the material, he walked backwards and stepped on a small child sitting on the front row. The child screamed and the Mayor, remaining dignified, turned and said, "Oh bugger, I'm sorry duck!" This was the most useful sentence he had spoken and it received the only discernible response of the entire morning.

The children left the hall and the Mayor was treated to his drink by Gillian. She invited him into the staff room and this was a most unpopular decision considering that it was now the morning break and the staff generally wanted some time to switch off. As the teachers sat down with a drink, the Mayor stood in a prominent position next to the microwave and cleared his throat, ready to speak. "I should like to say, ladies and gentlemen of the staff of this establishment, how honoured I am to have been invited to visit your school this morning." he announced. The staff looked up from their drinks and smiled grudgingly at this invasion of their coffee break. "I would like to say here and now that I always derive great pleasure from visiting schools and from meeting the fine people who make them possible. I know you will be as proud as I am when I say that I am very proud. I hold your children in very great esteem for the work they have done and I know you are equally proud on an equal basis as what I am. I hope your flag will remind you each day of the dedication of yourselves and your children in recycling the ozone."

"Can we just drink our coffee?" Paul requested politely. "It's knackering doing a Literacy Hour with a class like mine. I just want a minute's peace."

"Ah, the Literacy Hour. I know all about that because I attended one in a school last April. I would like to put it on record how much dedication is required to teach the Literacy Hour. It makes me very proud to see people carrying out such exciting learning experiences. When I was young there was no Literacy. It was all the three R's back then and when I look around at what happens now it makes me very proud. I'm so glad to a part of it."

Everyone studiously ignored him. They didn't want to talk shop. They didn't want to try and impress. They simply wanted a rest and a drink. And they desperately wanted the Mayor to piss off and leave them alone. The ignoring didn't work, however. He continued to give a speech until the break ended. Finally, when the room was empty, he concluded his oratory. He asked Gillian to show him the way to the Gents' and promptly disappeared through the door. As his wife waited outside, she watched Walt run up the corridor and burst into the Gents' behind her husband. Within seconds, Walt's voice could be heard through the door. "What do you think of this then? Have a good look. Have you ever seen anything like it? You don't get one like this through sitting on your arse and councilling. You have to work at something like this. Nah then." Mary, the Mayor's wife was listening intently, eyes wide open, hanging on every word that Walt spoke. "Touch it, go on, have a feel at that. It's perfection is that, there's not a fault in it. And don't think you're getting special favours on account of being Mayor because I'll tell you this and I'll tell you now, I've lost count of how many blokes I've taken into these toilets and I've yet to see one who's not speechless after seeing my little beauties." Mary – the alleged man muncher – was clearly desperate to get beyond that door. She felt she was missing something quite sensational, something she longed for all her life. "I've written to magazines, I have. I've asked 'em to do a feature but nobody's replied. It's perhaps a bit too specialist."

The door opened and the Mayor walked out, rather dazed, but this could have been due to inhaling in close proximity to Walt rather than from urinal overload. Mary smiled at Walt, emulating a twelve-year-old girl with a crush. Walt reciprocated with a nod and the enticing phrase, "Nah then!" As Jack and Mary were led to their car by Gillian, Mary rushed back inside to apparently check she had not left anything behind. She walked past Walt, slipped a piece of paper into his hand and turned once again to leave. The note contained the message Call Me 389467. Clearly, Walt was a babe magnet. His secret life of sex, drugs and sausage rolls was revealing itself. He looked at the note, farted and then commented, "What's she on about? Why does she want people to call her 389467? Mary's a lot easier to remember." And he screwed up the note and dropped it in a bin.

By the time I had waved the mayoral party off, Walt was on the phone to the planning department. The flagpole was causing him some concern and would preoccupy him for many weeks until the job was completed. His worries were being aired to the person on the other end of the line, whom I could only pray was not a nineteen year-old-girl. "I need to talk to you about me pole. Well, I think there's going to be some erection problems. It's a bloody big thing, you see, and I don't know how far it needs to be sunk in to counterbalance it. It's not going to be over-used, nah then. Once it's standing there I shall be running a flag up it once a week but not much more, apart from on special occasions. It's just that I don't want the bugger wobbling. Hello? Shit, they've cut me off."

"You did tell them you were talking about a flagpole, didn't you Walt!" I asked.

"Well, I told t'first person. I didn't tell that lass that you heard me talk to. I thought that first bloke would have said something."

I walked away, quietly smiling at the fact that we had won an award for energy conservation. In the five months since I arrived in September, I had used more energy than in the rest of my entire life!

Spring Term: Week 8

"There's two horses running round the field and Miss doesn't know what to do." The girl shouted, possibly in the mistaken belief that I *did* know what to do.

With the half term holiday behind us, we were on the run up to Easter. The weather would steadily improve, the children would spend fewer days stuck inside the building and the evenings would get lighter. After-school sports sessions would begin in a few more weeks and Walt would be a step closer each day to getting his pole up.

The new classroom was taking shape quite well. The walls were now built and today, the first Tuesday of the new half term, the roof girders were to be delivered. The new room had been designed with a flat roof so that it looked as crap as the original building. This had disappointed me at first and I remembered my early discussions with the architect in which he had proudly stated, "We'll make it match the existing building as closely as possible." And I had replied, "Oh, do you really have to!" However, the steel girders would be delivered this morning and by this afternoon they would be in place on top of the structure. After the roof was on, the work would move inside and it would begin to resemble a real classroom.

At nine forty-five, I heard the sound of the lorry in the yard and decided to go and take a look. Walt was already there when I arrived. He was telling the driver how to unload the roof girders from the lorry and giving the builders a few tips regarding the accurate fixing of the items to the basic structure. Nobody was listening.

When the girders were unloaded, the lorry drove away. Ladders were positioned at both sides of the new classroom and Mick the Foreman instructed his men in their task.

"Dave, you get up that far ladder. You're waiting up there till me and Bob pass this first girder across to you. You only need to slot it into that fixing bracket. It'll hold till we bolt it in." This all seemed satisfactory and actually quite simple, but I chose to stay and watch the first girder go into place. It seemed momentous in a pathetic sort of way. Walt nudged me and said, "They're doing it right. That's what I'd have suggested." His words gave me confidence that all was well.

Mick and Bob picked up the first girder and commented that it wasn't as heavy as that last bastard at their previous job. For this they were grateful and so with a spring in their step, they approached the ladder and climbed up, raising the girder as they went. A little jiggling was necessary to get the girder up to the very top, but soon it was resting on the front wall and a side wall of the new room. It would now be pushed in this diagonal position until it reached Dave. Upon reaching him, it would be positioned parallel with the front wall and fixed into position. Dave grabbed the girder when it approached him and pulled it sharply towards him.

"Oy, leave us a bit, you daft twat!" Mick suggested. He pulled the girder back slightly to his end of the room.

"Clever bastard!" Dave commented. "How am I supposed to get it in here?" He pulled the girder back to his fixing point.

"I telled yer, you dozy twat, you got too much at your end." Mick snapped, clearly pulling rank.

"Bollocks!" Dave replied respectfully.

Walt, standing beneath all this, shouted up to both men to inform them of his assessment of the situation. "Nah then, you're both a pair of soft wankers! From where I'm standing, this bloody girder's three inches too short. No wonder you're playing bloody tug o' war with it. You want to work it out, you daft pancakes. I'll leave it with you!"

He was right. The girder was slightly too short to span the roof. Mick and his men carried it back down and laid it alongside the other girders in the batch. All twelve were exactly the same length. All twelve were too short. "Bollocks!" Mick announced. The other gentlemen nodded their heads in agreement with Mick's profound comment upon the proceedings. "How can they be too bloody short?" Mick asked.

"Ah, well they're not long enough, you see!" Walt interjected with mathematical precision. "It's down to your measurements, nah then. Your measurements are different to what you gave these here manufacturers. So they've made 'em too short. You should have telled 'em right. I'll tell you this and I'll tell you now and I'll tell you reight and straight and when it's said it's said, this'll add to your bill and no mistake. Nah then. You'll have to have these buggers taken back and have some more made. That'll cost you more than a packet of Ginger Nuts."

"Walt, piss off!" Mick politely requested.

"Well I will. I've got things to do to my pipework. I'll leave it with you."

I walked back inside the building as a rather deflated Mick took out his mobile phone and began admitting that there was a problem. To his team, there was no immediate worry – it meant the kettle could go on earlier than anticipated and this was an unexpected bonus.

By the time I was approaching my office, Walt was in a toilet and could be heard grumbling furiously. "Are you OK in there, Walt?" I shouted through the door.

"You might well ask, and since you did ask, no I'm not. Not now I've found this. Nah then."

"Why? What have you found?"

"It's that bloody new cleaner, Joan." He replied, somewhat confusingly.

"She's not in there, is she? She's not supposed to start work for another three hours." I opened the door and joined Walt, who was on his back with his knees in the air and his head and shoulders wedged behind a sink pedestal.

"I just decided to do a quick inspection as I came past. And I'll tell you this and I'll tell you now, she's not been keeping to my standards of bog cleanliness. It's a disgrace behind this sink. This is where your germs breed. We'll get kids catching tripoid and hypothermia if we go on like this. Shall I tell you what I've just found? Shall I tell you? I will. I'll tell you. I've just happened to lay on my back down here and I've come face to face with t'biggest dead beetle I've ever seen. It were just lying here."

"They do that, Walt, dead beetles."

"Nah then, you should see t'size of it!"

"It's big, is it?"

"Put it this way, if you come across a dead beetle bigger than this it'll be called John Lennon. I'll be having words with her tonight. I told her she's to polish these bogs till she can see her face in 'em and I know it's hard for her to tell on account of her having a face like a turd, but she's not making an effort. I shall be needing you to back me up when she gets here."

"Fair enough, Walt."

"It's a slippery slope when your toilet hygiene system fails. I'd go so far as to say it's an elf and safety. And when the shit hits the fan it'll all come down on my head. I'll not be wanting it. I'll leave it with you."

I pencilled a note in my diary to remind me to talk to Joan, although I didn't really expect to get a word in edgeways.

I heard the sound of children in the corridors. They were setting off outside for their morning break and things seemed perfectly normal. The corridors quietened as the last of the children departed and various members of staff passed my office on the way to the staff room. Suddenly, with an urgency normally associated with leaving the building at the end of the day, a girl ran along the corridor and banged furiously on my door. "Sir! Sir! Come outside, quickly. We need you outside. Mrs. Short doesn't know what to do!"

"What's the matter?" I asked as I set off along the corridor with the girl. "Is someone hurt?"

"Not yet. At least they weren't when I came in."

"What's happening out there?" I asked, now in a state of panic. I had a fear that a machete-wielding madman might be racing round the playground, slicing limbs off small children as he went.

"It's the two horses." Came her reply.

"The two horses?" I repeated slowly.

"They're running round the field and Miss doesn't know what to do." She confirmed, possibly in the mistaken belief that I *did* know what to do.

I ran quickly to the staff room and asked for someone to urgently phone the RSPCA and the police. I presumed the horses were the ones that lived in a field adjacent to the school field and so I asked if someone could have an attempt at contacting the owner. I then bolted out of the building to survey the state of play.

As described very accurately by the young girl, the horses were careering around the field, rearing and bucking as they did so. At the moment, the children on the yard were well out of danger range but that could change in seconds. I asked Celia to get the children inside as calmly as possible and in response, she took out her whistle and blew it hard. The children stopped and so, to my horror did the horses on the field. I told the children to walk in through the nearest door and they began to do so. And then the horses also began to move. They began running towards the playground and my heart started pounding.

"Nice and quickly, everybody!" I called out, trying to appear calm. "Straight inside, quick as you can."

The horses were bounding across the field in our direction. Their manner was playful but I was well aware that their strength could be lethal to a small child. I ushered the children in through the doors. Celia did the same. Some older children began helping the younger ones. They could tell the situation was potentially dangerous. They knew the need to protect the little ones was becoming urgent. As the last few children were squeezing through the doors, the horses appeared on the playground. With loud snorting noises they ran and jumped almost uncontrollably until eventually one of the horses kicked out at a metal fence section that made up the boundary to the builders' compound. The fence was flung into the air like a rag and then came crashing down within inches of the builders' tea-break caravan.

The door of the caravan opened and revealed the faces of Mick the Foreman and, surprisingly, Walt who had been partaking of a crafty cuppa. "What the bloody hell were that!" was Walt's highly appropriate question. This was answered immediately by the creature itself as it now began to race towards the caravan. Being surprised by the sight of a large stallion coming towards him at an uncomfortable velocity, Walt emitted the cry of "Shit, it's a

bleeding hoss!" This prompted the other gentlemen to come and
observe and upon spotting the horse, they had to admit that Walt had
made a truly accurate assessment.

"That's a big bugger!" Mick announced.

"Aye, and it's coming right at us!" Bob said.

"Shit!" Dave added, poignantly.

The horse ran frighteningly close to the caravan and then
stopped in its tracks, turned and bucked its way across the yard.
Assuming the coast was clear the four men left the caravan in order
to avoid a second trouser-soiling incident. Ensuring the horse was
heading towards the field they turned to run the other way and came,
somewhat unexpectedly, face to face with the second beast. Mick,
attempting to say that he had been hitherto unaware of the existence
of a second horse, issued forth the phrase, "Bollocks, there's another
bugger! Run!" His team followed his instructions to the letter and
between them they fled in every manageable direction, with the
possible exception of 'up'.

With the children safely inside and the building team now
fully aware that things were taking an unusual turn, I felt a little less
worried about the general safety surrounding the situation. But I still

had two large horses charging frantically around, churning up the field and clomping across the concrete yard. I was worried that a horse might kick out at a window and shower a crowd of children with glass, but I had no idea what to do to take control of the situation.

And then Gillian appeared. This was the challenge she had waited for. Her quest for total power had been waning a little over recent months as she already wielded a reign of terror over the children, staff and parents in the school. This had clearly left her with a sense of dissatisfaction as there was nobody new for her to begin terrifying on a daily basis, but now she had the opportunity to gain control of a pair of wild horses. If she could win this fight, what chance would an angry parent or miscreant child have against her!

A large woman in both stature and personality, she looked quite ridiculous bounding out of the door dressed in her red anorak and holding three skipping ropes that had been procured from the PE store and tied together. She marched towards the field with purposeful strides.

"Gillian, don't do anything dangerous!" I called out.

"I've got to do something! Nobody else is planning to do anything!" she shouted back. She looked towards the horses and shouted, "Hey, come here at once!" but they rather surprisingly ignored her. This, I feared, was a foolish move on the part of the two fine beasts, as Gillian expected to be obeyed at all times. She gave a snort, not dissimilar to those of the horses, and began to run at full pelt onto the field, swinging her skipping ropes above her head. These had now become a lasso and I feared that the Wild West was not yet ready for Gillian and her forthright ways of dealing with problems.

Walt had watched the event unfold with interest, but from behind a tree. He now felt the need to offer advice and words of caution. "Nah then, you bloody pancake, come back!" he called. "You don't reason with hosses. They'll trample you!"

"I don't reason with anybody!" Gillian replied, quite correctly. "They'll do as they're told." She continued charging across the grass as Walt cried out the phrase 'bloody pancake' several times in vain. She swung the rope in an attempt to ensnare the first horse, but she missed. The horse ran towards the playground once more and Gillian followed it, her red anorak streaking by as I watched. The builders, on seeing the horse and Gillian approach the playground, helped by shouting, "Shit, it's coming back, get behind a bloody wall."

"Hide!" shouted Dave.

"Aye, don't let it see you. It might kick!" yelled Bob.

"Bugger the horse! I mean hide from her!" shouted Dave. "If she sees us, she'll make us help her!" The men, seeing much sense in this viewpoint, hid rapidly.

As the horse turned back to the field, Gillian swung her lariat once more and this time it landed with amazing precision around the horse's neck. The speed of the horse was a little greater than Gillian had anticipated and she was pulled from her feet and dragged some considerable distance in the muddy grass. Walt, emerged from behind his tree and, in an attempt to save Gillian from danger, threw his immense bulk on top of her as she passed. This new ballast was too much for the horse and, I suspected, rather a lot for Gillian, to sustain. The horse slowed down and stopped.

There was now an imprint in the mud. It marked the spot where Walt had mounted Gillian and compressed her body into the field. As Gillian peeled herself from this crater, she was hardly recognisable, being covered from head to toe, and possibly beyond, in dark, sticky mud. She seized upon the moment, however, and whilst the horse was still a little puzzled, she led it smartly to the edge of the field where she could corner it and tie it to a strong tree.

"Grand job, lass!" Walt remarked. "Sorry about jumping on you! I wouldn't normally jump on anybody on account of I'm a bit overweight and it could hurt. But then I thought, bugger it, she's an 'efty lass herself, she'll manage."

"Thank you, Walt." Gillian said grudgingly. "But there's no time for chatting. Go and get that other horse whilst I keep an eye on this one."

"Me? I can't go and get you no hoss. I'll end up trampled. I'll be as flat as a bloody pancake, you bloody pancake."

"I thought you were a man, Walt. How come I can do it when you can't?" Gillian barked.

"Aye, well, you might ask and since you did ask, I'll tell you. You're more of a bloody man than all t'rest of us put together. I'll tell you that and I'll tell you now and I'll leave it with you. I'm not going after one of them things wi' just a skipping rope, nah then."

"Fear! They can smell fear. They know I'm not scared so they respond." She growled.

"Aye, well, I *am* scared. I'm scared of being trampled by an 'oss and I'm shit scared of buggers like you!"

In all honesty, the other horse had lost its sense of excitement now that its partner was back in harness. It wandered slowly around the field, stopping to munch grass every few steps. Within a few more minutes the owner of the horses arrived, having been successfully contacted by Ann. He backed his horse box onto the yard and calmly led the two creatures into it. "They're perfectly safe." He announced. "They get a little over-excited, but they're perfectly safe."

"I'll tell you this and I'll tell you now and I'll tell you reight and straight and when it's said it's said and I'll say no more, they're not safe." Walt informed him. "They're not safe when that bloody pancake's chasing 'em around t'field! No bugger's safe when she's on her high hoss!" he indicated Gillian as he spoke. "But I'll tell you this, I'd pay you handsomely for one of them there tranquilliser darts. She could do with one of them up her arse on a daily basis, she could."

"Well done, Gillian." I said with a smile. "But just remember, you're only human and we don't want to see you ending up in hospital."

"Human?" she said with a huge grin becoming visible beneath the mud. "If you let a rumour like that get around it'll ruin my credibility."

"Do you want to go and get a change of clothes? I'll look after your class."

"No! It'll stop the kids from coming too close if I stay like this. Just keep an eye on them whilst I wash my face."

I couldn't help admiring her. She was over-the-top, bombastic, dogmatic and sometimes downright vicious. But I couldn't help admiring her. But I tried not to dwell on it for too long.

Spring Term: Week 9

From his central, elevated position in the hall, he successfully managed to scatter the contents of his stomach over nine children who were seated nearby. The chaos that ensued was legendary.

At seven o'clock on Tuesday morning I had a phone call from Alan. "Sorry about this, but feeling a bit poorly!" he announced. "Chucking up for quite a while in the night, still not over it. Think I'm going to need the day off. Can't stand up in front of a class if I'm having to keep vomiting. I don't like being ill, I'm not a good patient."

"Don't worry Alan. Take the day off and see how you feel. Give us a ring this afternoon to let us know the situation for tomorrow."

"Thanks a lot. Much appreciated. Don't know what it is, normally I'm quite resistant to…Got to go, vomiting!"

I decided to skip breakfast and set off early. Trying to find a supply teacher at short notice was hard work and I figured I needed to be in my office as quickly as possible with my list of names. If I could ring a teacher before another school did, we might be in luck. But as I picked up my car keys the phone rang again. This time it was Amanda Chaplin. "I don't think I can come in today." She groaned. "I've got some horrible sickness bug. I can't stop throwing up. I don't think I'd even make the journey, never mind stand in front of a class. I'm ever so sorry."

"Don't worry Amanda, we'll get it covered. You have a good rest and give us a ring later on." This was now a good reason to panic. If I was unable to get supply teachers I would have immense difficulty teaching one class of seven-year-olds and one class of eleven-year-olds at the same time.

As I replaced the handset, the phone rang again. Celia Short's husband was on the line informing me that she had been ill all night and wasn't fit to come into work. I thanked him for his call and wondered whether to celebrate the day's events by cracking open a vein.

I eventually arrived in my office and after an hour and twenty minutes of phone calls I managed to secure supply teachers for each of the three classes. Two would be in school within a quarter of an hour. The third, having a long distance to travel would not arrive until nine forty-five but this didn't matter to me – she could come and that was the extent of my concern. I was happy to cover Alan's class until the supply teacher arrived.

Alan's class was strangely depleted. As I registered them I found that eight children were absent and I began to wonder if their complaint was the same as Alan's. Not that I expected them to have grown a beard and undergone a personality extraction, of course. It was simply that I wondered if they had a sickness bug. If so, how many others throughout the school might be suffering similarly?

The arrival of the supply teacher gave me an opportunity to go and find out. As soon as the lady, whose name was Vicky, had walked through the door of the classroom I attempted to make my departure. She appeared to want to tell me about her love of Morris Dancing but I quickly, and rather feebly, explained that I would probably fall off the roof of any car that I tried to dance on, and left. Back at the office, all hell had broken loose. The bug had infiltrated the entire school. It was an epidemic. It was the Plague revisited. There were seventeen children sitting outside Ann's office waiting for their parents to collect them. The small number of buckets that were usually available for vomiting children clearly could not cope with this unprecedented demand and the sight of the ashen faced children, sitting three-to-a-bucket did nothing for the equanimity of one's own stomach. I was glad that I had skipped breakfast.

Ann was in a flap. A line of children throwing up outside her office and the immediate need to contact their parents did not replace her usual work, it simply added a rather unpleasant dimension to it. The endless phone calls from the LEA and company sales staff continued, as did the need to calculate the numbers of children requiring lunch today. This information needed to be given to the cook as quickly as possible so that she could set to work.

"I'm not enjoying this!" Ann informed me. "I don't know what it is but they're throwing up like rabbits. And those four on the end of the line might be with us all day. I can't get a reply from anybody on their contact lists."

"OK, keep trying. I'll sort out the numbers for the cook."

Amidst the background cacophony of retching and coughing, another child appeared at the office door. Aged about six, this boy announced the reason for his appearance in a loud voice. "Miss has sent me 'cos I keep puking." He informed us. "I've done it all over me maths book." I looked down the line of children and, upon being struck with the realisation that there was no current bucket availability, I rushed to Walt's store to obtain a receptacle for the boy to vomit into. The sight of an additional bucket brought a moment of joy to the vomiting children who could now calculate that a further three or four could join their ranks at no detriment to those who had already secured a bucket. Ann approached the boy to ask for contact information.

"Can you tell me your phone number?" she asked.

"It begins with four." He responded quite positively.

"Do you know the rest of it?"

"No."

She returned to her computer to run a search. Sometimes, asking the children could be quicker than looking on the computer. Clearly, sometimes it wasn't. She found the number. As the boy had stated, it began with a four. The number was 576390. The telephone claimed that this number was not recognised.

"I can't get any reply from your number, dear. It says it's not been recognised." Ann told the boy.

"Yeah. That's 'cos we've been cut off." He replied in a very cool manner before vomiting noisily into the bucket.

"Does anyone at home have a mobile?" she asked him.

"No."

"Do you have a neighbour we could phone?"

"They don't talk to us. Nobody on our street talks to us. It's since me mum got pissed and put bricks through all their windows one night." He ratified this latter statement by throwing up once more into the bucket. He then proceeded to describe the contents of the bucket to anyone within earshot and this prompted seven other children to begin vomiting profusely into their shared buckets with a heart-warming display of co-operation.

Three parents arrived and upon entering the building, sniffed in a curious manner. They collected four of the children and led them staggering weakly down the drive. I ventured to the kitchen with my offering of the approximate dinner numbers for the cook. "The numbers are not going to be right, Diane!" I told her. "The kids are dropping like flies. I'm not sure there'll be any left by lunchtime! So this is the current state of play. But honestly, I don't know how many more kids will have gone home by twelve o'clock."

"Well, I can do without this!" she snapped.

"We can all do without it!" I replied. "But there's not a lot we can do about it."

"I could end up with a wastage! Catering Department don't like it when there's a wastage. They'll be on my back!"

"Pass them on to me if they complain. I'll vouch for you. It's nobody's fault, is it! It's just one of those things."

"I've got a delivery of ice cream, jelly and hundreds and thousands coming today. If there's not enough kids to eat it, I can't store my ice cream. I'm short on freezer space."

I desperately wanted to ask her what quantities she ordered 'hundreds and thousands' in, but I left instead. I had an assembly to do.

The children filed into the hall for their assembly. They came in class by class and sat down in rows. The hall usually became very crowded during an assembly. The oldest children sat at the back and whispered to each other all the way through, the youngest ones sat at the front and never stayed still. A small space remained at the front for me to stand. If I tried to walk I would invariably trip over the legs of a small child and so I tended to remain in one place. Today, however, there seemed to be more room than usual. With about forty children missing from the hall, either because they were absent or because they were throwing up outside Ann's office, it all felt surprisingly spacious. I allowed myself a little more room at the front of the hall by pushing the remaining two hundred and seventy children back a short way.

As was normally the case, a child would annoy someone during the assembly and this would annoy me. Today it was the turn of Christopher Matthews, an extremely irritating boy in Year Three. He was sitting in the exact centre of the hall and was poking other children, much to their annoyance.

"Christopher Matthews, stand up!" I shouted. He stood up and I informed him that he was to remain standing for the duration of the assembly so that I could see what he was doing. He looked like an obelisk, tall and thin, in the very centre of the room, with a sea of seated children around him. The punishment clearly worked because he could no longer mess around. Indeed, he looked a little subdued and this was most unlike him. I had no inkling that the curious look on his face was to cause me more trouble than a mere poking attack had previously done.

The subdued expression was due to an uncomfortable feeling in his stomach. With no warning, either for the benefit of himself or for others, Christopher suddenly emitted a loud belch and began to vomit profusely. From his central, elevated position in the hall, he successfully managed to scatter the contents of his stomach over nine children who were seated nearby. The chaos that ensued was legendary. The children who had been vomited upon leapt up in horror, brushing Christopher's breakfast off their clothes and not particularly worrying about where it went. Consequently, the fall out from Christopher's stomach began to contaminate a much larger proportion of the group. For those children who were already struggling with a slightly upset stomach, this was all too much. The sight and smell of Christopher's regurgitation sent their own stomach muscles into involuntary contraction. At least ten children began throwing up, each heaving and spewing a little more than the last, as if hoping for recognition and a certificate if they proved to be the best.

Sick was flying everywhere. There was scarcely a child in the hall untouched by a passing fragment of vomit as it projected from a nearby mouth or was brushed from a nearby sleeve. The floor became covered with foul-smelling gunge and this prompted yet more children to display the contents of their stomachs. Even those who had arrived at school feeling healthier than a lap dancer's bank balance had now developed a queasiness and uncertainty in the abdomen. Previously fit children who could no longer stand the sights and smells prevalent in today's act of collective worship, began joining their ailing compatriots, throwing up wherever space allowed.

In the midst of this chaos I rushed to the nearby staff room and asked for help in getting the children outside and into the fresh air. As the staff came to help I noticed two of them had ventured forth whilst eating a piece of ginger cake. I warned them against taking this to the hall and for a moment they looked puzzled. And then the smell drifted into their nostrils and the cake was returned rapidly.

Removing the children from the hall was a fearsome task. Whilst many were still throwing up, we sent the children out, class by class, each child being forced to wade through puddles of half-digested corn flakes, porridge and various indiscriminate items. The vomiting continued onto the corridor as the children left the hall. At times, when a group of children reached a bottleneck on their journey, someone would have no option but to vomit down someone else's back, thus sparking off a chain reaction of a truly horrible kind.

The task of contacting close to one hundred and fifty parents was going to be a mammoth one. We would have to contact not only the parents of the vomit*ers*, but also those of the vomit*ees*, those who had been puked upon and were now walking around in repulsively encrusted school uniforms. I decided to tell Ann that any parent she contacted should be asked to bring along any other parent that they happened to live near, or pass on their way to school. We needed to get as many children out of the building as possible so that we could deal with those whose parents could not be reached.

The hall floor was one of the most revolting sights I had ever seen. It was a multi-coloured mosaic of repugnance. As I stood and tried to think how to tackle it, I heard Walt's Jeep race up the drive as he returned from his break. His day was about to be ruined beyond all imagination. He opened the door and caught sight of me. "Nah then!" was his greeting. This was followed by a sniff and the comment of, "Bleeding hell! Summat smells bad in here. I hope I've not got a blockage. I can do without a blockage today, I've got a lot to do. I'd better check me urinals. I'll be back in half an hour."

"Walt!" I shouted. "You've not got a blockage. Neither have about two hundred kids. We've had a throwing up session in the hall. It's a serious mess."

"You've had a what? You've had 'em throwing up? These bloody modern education methods get dafter! What do you need to teach 'em to throw up for?"

"No Walt. We're not teaching them. We've got a bug going round. They've all got it. One of them started in the assembly and it set them all off. I'll give you a hand to get it cleaned up."

"No, it's alright, I'll manage." He said as he walked to the hall. Upon reaching it, however, he had a slight change of heart. "Bloody hell! Oh now that's revolting! I think I might ask you to help, if you don't mind. It turns your stomach, does this!"

The though of Walt's sizeable stomach turning filled me with dread. With such a vast cubic capacity I feared that this was a man who would have been a veritable asset to the Dambusters, had he been around at the time. Not that he would have been the bouncing bomb. No, they would have simply needed to unleash his stomach contents over the city to have completed their task. I hoped beyond all doubt that this environment did not make him feel queasy.

"I'll be back in a minute. I'm not feeling so good." He announced, thus proving that there was a God – and he hated me. True to his word, he was back in a very short time, although whether this was an actual minute was open to debate. "Well that's me buggered. I reckon I'll have that bloody blockage now!" he informed me. " I'll have to get me drain rods out. It were that tikka masala. Indians never agree with me, except for that Amit lad who lives next door but three. I get on well with him. I thought I felt funny before I came this morning but it weren't sickness. It were constipation. I suffer from that a lot, I do. I went to tell me doctor but he couldn't give a shit. I suppose I can't either – that's me problem."

We set to work with mops and buckets, steadily returning the hall floor to its original state. A line of children remained outside Ann's office whilst she tried to contact parents. From time to time the awful sound of retching could be heard along the corridor and we knew that our task of floor cleaning was a long way from its completion. Gradually, various parents arrived and collected either children with washed out faces, or alternatively, children who needed their clothes to be washed out. Many asked to borrow a bucket in order to protect the interior of the car but understood immediately when Ann pointed to the many, many children sharing the tiny number of buckets.

Oblivious to all this, Diane the cook emerged from the kitchen at eleven fifteen. She found Walt and me cleaning the hall floor. She sniffed, smelling something unsavoury in the air, and tapped me on the shoulder. "Do you think them numbers will be right then, or what?" she asked in a rather aggressive tone.

"I think they'll be more wrong than they've ever been in the history of educational catering since early Roman times." I replied.

"What's that mean? Are they right or wrong?" she growled.

"Wrong!" I affirmed.

"Wrong?" she questioned.

"Right!"

"Make your bloody mind up. Which is it?" She was never hard to confuse. That was the very reason I did it.

"Wrong." I nodded.

"Wrong." She repeated.

"Right!" I said again, just for devilment.

"Why are they wrong? It's not hard to count how many kids are here and look at how many stay for dinner."

"Not on a normal day it isn't. But the kids that were here this morning when the registers were filled in, by and large aren't here now. And the ones that are still here don't necessarily want to eat anything."

"Well, why can't somebody come and tell me if a kid goes home? It's not like fifty of 'em have buggered off, is it!"

"No, Diane. It's more like a hundred and fifty."

"Well I'd have liked to have known. I mean if you've got time to help Walt do his job, surely you could pop through and tell me some kids have gone home." I scowled and as I did so, she walked round to the other side of me. I presumed she wished to give my other ear a similar onslaught and was grateful for her fairness. Bracing myself for a further attack I was surprised to hear the words, "Jesus, what the bloody hell have I just trodden in!"

"Oh, that'll be the vomit." I replied.

"Vomit?"

"Sick. Puke. Partially digested stomach contents. That's what we're cleaning up. That's why I'm helping Walt. There was a lake in here half an hour ago – and it's still all over the corridors. That might be why I forgot to come through and tell you the numbers had altered."

"It's on me shoes. I can't go back in my kitchen with sick on me shoes."

Walt, overhearing this comment, aquaplaned gracefully across to Diane. "You're bloody right. Don't you set foot in that kitchen with sick on your shoes or you'll have an elf and safety. It'll be viramental elf, that will. I know about these things and you'll not be wanting a viramental elf."

"I'll not be wanting bloody sick on me shoes, neither."

"Stick 'em outside and I'll hose 'em down, nah then. But it'll not be till I've got all t'puke off them corridors so I'll leave it with you."

Walt did a sterling job of cleaning the floors and of hosing down Diane's shoes. His personal aroma once again quickly cancelled out all traces of the pungent smell that had earlier infiltrated every nook and cranny of the hall. The smell of Diane's cooking wafted through and blended interestingly with Walt's after shave and her sweet voice could be heard remarking that she had made a hundred and fifty lunches and there were only sixty-one children to eat them. This, she pointed out at least sixteen times in my hearing, meant wastage. I was inclined to agree. The waste of words was unforgivable.

Just seven children were now left outside Ann's office. Five of them had a telephone number in common on their contact lists. It was the number of Rosemary, the child minder from Hartwell Street. Each of the five children was dropped off in the morning by Rosemary and picked up in the evening by Rosemary. At some point after being picked up, they did – I was led to believe – come into brief contact with their parents. Each set of parents had given specific instructions that we should only ever contact Rosemary during the day. The jobs of the parents were far too important for them to be bothered by accidents or illnesses suffered by their children. No, things that required care and attention were Rosemary's department. The parents confined themselves to providing money and toys as these were widely known to be far more important than love.

Rosemary had been incommunicado throughout the morning. The sight of these obviously very poorly children suggested to me that we try Rosemary once more and if she could not be contacted, we would ring the parents whether they liked it or not. The children were far too ill to be at school. Ann tried Rosemary's number once more, and this time there was an answer. As ever, I listened, open mouthed, to Ann's description of the situation. "Hello dear, it's Ann at the school. Yes that's right. How are you? Oh that's good. Now I'm going to have to ask you to come up to school, it's sickness I'm afraid. Which one? Well, all of them. Yes that's right, the lot. We've lost well over a hundred children. Well, when I say 'lost', I mean 'sent home'. We've not lost any in the sense of disappearing. Or dying for that matter. But all five of yours have been vomiting furiously. They still are in fact. I don't know where it all comes from, well, of course, it comes from their stomachs, but you know what I mean. Poor little mites, they've had to share a bucket because we've not got enough. Well, you don't expect more than two or three throwing up at any one time, do you? Now I can't lend you a bucket or anything so if you've got one it might be a good idea to bring it up. Yes, well we've had everything else brought up today so you might as well. I'll see you soon then." She put the phone down and told me that Rosemary didn't sound terribly excited at the prospect of collecting five incessant pukers. I couldn't understand why that should be!

The remaining two children were from families who had no means of contact. One was the boy whose phone was cut off, another was a girl for whom we had tried every number and failed. The sad little specimens sat and watched the other children disappear one by one, to go home to a comfortable bed. The two children knew that they would still be here at the end of the day, feeling terribly ill but taking solace in the knowledge that they could at least enjoy the luxury of puking in their very own bucket.

I almost made the mistake of thinking that things were gradually getting back to normal, when I felt an uncomfortable gurgling in my stomach. I wondered whether to sit outside Ann's office with a bucket whilst she telephoned my mother but in the event, after far too many sudden and impromptu trips to the gents, I went home and remained there until Thursday.

Spring Term: Week 10

First rule of Health and Safety…

It had taken some time this morning to pacify Walt. His wife had recently bought a book on plants and he had been skimming through it during a moment of boredom at home. Vaguely recollecting a photograph from the book, he became convinced that the geranium growing outside the staff room window was in fact cannabis. He rightly informed me that if the school should be found to be growing its own cannabis then things would go to pot. We were not growing cannabis, but my attempts to allay his fears were like seeds set upon tarmac. He was utterly convinced that his identification of the plant was accurate. After all, he had skimmed the two hundred-page plant book for more than three minutes. "I'm telling you, it's that marjiwanka stuff." He insisted. "I'll tell you this and I'll tell you now, these addictive types can smell that stuff a mile away. They'll be down here, stuffing it into syringes and injecting it into their armpits. I know what they get up to. Mrs. Eccles down our street, her son's girlfriend's brother started doing marjiwanka and methane. So I know what I'm talking about."

"Walt, it was planted by the council. They don't go round schools planting cannabis. They're not even allowed to plant stuff that prickles nowadays. Stop worrying." I pleaded.

"Well, if it is that marjiwanka, it'll be on your head. I'm having nowt to do wi' it. I'm not having some bugger excusing me of growing cannabis, so put that in your pipe and smoke it. I'm sorry if I sound bolshy, but I have principalities when it comes to drugs. Nah then."

I caught sight of movement outside my office window. Fearing the arrival of a gang of geranium sniffers I turned sharply to check the identity of my new visitors. In the event it was a single visitor. It was Ian Jacobs, the local authority Health and Safety Officer. I hadn't arranged for him to visit so I had to assume he was either at the wrong school, or else he was here for a spot check. Walt was emitting venom from his gaze as he watched the man walk toward the door. "It's that elf and safety bloke!" he informed me. "He'd better not be coming here!" As the school drive was half a mile long and the man had passed two signs displaying the school's name, I rather assumed that he might be 'coming here', but I secretly hoped he had made a mistake.

"Good morning! Sorry to drop in like this but I want to have a quick look round." Ian announced with a smile.

"Right. I didn't know you were coming." I told him.

"No. I tend to just turn up. I get a better picture of things that way. You can spare me an hour, can't you!"

"It looks like it. Come in."

"Not until I've signed in. First rule of health and safety, always know who you've got in your building."

Ian was a curious fellow. He was short and stocky with black hair that never moved – just like the kind you find on an Action Man doll. His life revolved around health and safety and he found it impossible to walk into a room without modifying it in some way. I often felt that if he had his way, the world would be made of foam rubber so that nobody, however careless, could injure themselves. I had argued once before with the man about this very point. I felt it was good for children to sometimes learn that things could be dangerous. It helped them to become more careful in my view. I felt that if children were too well protected against injury, they would possibly not realise that dangers existed. This, I thought, could be potentially disastrous when they grew up. But he did not agree and I had fears that he might order the new classroom to be knocked down and replaced with a bouncy castle.

I tried to imagine this man on a beach, measuring the force with which the tide came in to see if it was safe to paddle in. Or perhaps he would check the diameter of the sand grains to ensure they could not become a choking hazard. I pitied his children on their holiday. Of course, he might never take them on holiday. The roads might be too bumpy, the aeroplane might have a dodgy reading lamp, or he might not feel able to lift his luggage without the proper hoisting equipment, having referred to Section twenty-three of his Manual Handling manual. And then my thoughts drifted to the aforementioned document. If it was big and heavy, should there be a manual to explain how to handle the Manual Handling manual? If so, would it be called the Manual Handling Manual Handling Manual? Should it be available on a disc? I felt it should, as an electronic Manual Handling manual would be lighter than a manual Manual Handling manual. I suddenly became aware that he was looking at me. I had missed every word he had spoken.

It appeared that he wished to walk round the school with Walt and me. Walt was required due to his role as Site Manager. I was required due to my role of 'anything that goes wrong is my fault'. But as I reached for a clipboard to help me look interested I caught sight of Ian staring at Ann whilst she worked on her computer. It could, I pondered, be a case of love at first sight, but then he took a sharp intake of breath and shook his head. Ann became aware of his interest in either her, or what she was doing, and stopped work, feeling quite awkward.

"I don't like what I see." Ian said.

"She can't help it. She always looks like that." I replied.

"No, no. Look at the way that computer is set up on the desk. The monitor is offset, I would say about twenty degrees to the right. She has to turn her head to look at it. First rule of health and safety, always be totally comfortable. Repetitive strain injury waiting to happen. Let's get it sorted out."

I was beginning to suffer from 'repetitive strain', having heard this man repeat the phrase 'first rule of health and safety' twice since he had arrived and wondering how many more first rules there might be. However, I watched him make drastic changes to

Ann's workstation. Her keyboard, directly in front of her, was left alone. Ian's problem was with the monitor, which sat on top of the computer processor. In order for this to fit on the desk, it had to be offset slightly to Ann's right. She liked it this way because it allowed her to see out of the window ahead of her. But Ian made Ann stand up and placed the monitor on her chair. Then, in a tangle of wires, he lowered the processor to the floor, standing it on its edge beneath Ann's desk. He placed the monitor directly in Ann's line of vision and smiled in a satisfied sort of way. "That should sort out your problem." He announced.

"But I didn't have a problem." Ann protested.

"Believe me, you did. First rule of health and safety, always be on the lookout for potential problems."

Having done the good deed, we left Ann and progressed through the school. Entering the first classroom, I asked Gillian to excuse us whilst Ian took a look round. Gillian's class of six-year-olds stopped what they were doing and stared intently at Ian as he walked around the room inspecting the floor, worktops, shelves and the state of the chairs. A little girl watched him as he approached her, eyes fixed on a cable that trailed along the skirting board. "Have you lost something?" She asked him.

"No." he replied.

"What yer looking for then?" she persisted.

"Nothing, I'm just looking."

"How can you be just looking if you're not looking for anything?"

"I'm looking for things that might be dangerous."

"Rottweilers are dangerous. My Auntie Jade's got one."

"Yes, well, I don't think I'm likely to find a rottweiler here, am I!" He was clearly fed up of this child and attempted to walk away quickly. She got out of her seat and followed him.

"Volcanoes are dangerous too!" she explained to him. "They burst open and lager comes out. It's called corrupting, me dad told me."

"I'm not looking for volcanoes!" he snapped.

"Good, 'cos we haven't got one. You can borrow my rubber if you like."

"Why would I want to do that?" he asked.

"If you've lost yours."

"But I haven't. I haven't lost anything." Except his patience, I mused.

He walked rapidly to the front of the room whilst Gillian told the girl to sit down and do her work. Seemingly happy with the condition of the room, he made to leave but stopped by a shelf near the doorway. He took out a tape measure and shook his head. "Bit dodgy, this. It's just at the right height to bump your head on. And it looks like the brackets are a bit loose. First rule of health and safety, tight brackets." He shook the shelf as if to prove a point. The bracket at the other end of the shelf slipped out of position and the shelf began to fall. The books on the shelf slid away from Ian rapidly and landed on a small child sitting at the closest desk. As the books rained down on the child, the little boy leapt up from his seat. His head collided with the chin of a girl who had stood up to see what was happening and she began to cry with gusto. The boy fell backwards over his chair, grasping the desk for help, but this simply caused him to pull it over so that it landed on both his own legs and another boy's toes. I wanted to make a 'first rule of health and safety' comment but refrained.

We left Gillian and walked into Amanda's classroom. Amanda, looking up from working with a child, immediately called out, "Thanks for coming. She's sitting over there."

"Pardon?" I said.

"Pardon?" Ian said.

"Tha what, duck?" Walt said.

"Oh, er, I thought you were Sarah's dad. He's coming to collect her. She's not very well." Amanda explained. "But you're not, are you!" I went to tell Amanda who the visitor was and she asked if I could get him to condemn the children as serious health hazards. I promised to try but warned her to not hold out much hope. When I returned to Ian, he was tugging at the carpet and telling Walt that it needed to be more securely fixed at the doorway.

"Well it does now, you pancake, 'cos you've pulled it up. I can't get that stuck down till all these here kids have gone home. So now, instead of it being a little bit ruffled, it's stuck up three bloody miles so that any bugger can fall over it. We've got people in and out of here all day. Pancake." Ian assured Walt that it wouldn't be a problem if Amanda told all the children to be careful. Walt assured Ian that the kids would forget. Walt then assured me that Ian was a pillock, but I already knew that. I decided that I would tell the children immediately and asked them to stop what they were doing so that they could listen.

"Now children, over near the door…" I had spoken just six words when June, a classroom assistant returned from her mission. Her mission had been to acquire an overhead projector in readiness for the next lesson and she had accomplished this with honours, returning as she was with the bulky machine. Now, approaching the classroom door and with the entire class looking in that direction, she became entangled with the carpet. She lost her footing and began to fall forward, flinging the heavy – not to mention expensive – machine out of her grasp. It bounced onto the floor with a sickening rattle, suggesting to me that all was not well within. The glass atop the projector shattered and small shards came to rest in the carpet around a table of six children who now resembled the unfortunate members of a less than successful knife-throwing act.

Ian looked embarrassed. "I presume your department will pay for a new projector!" I suggested in a menacing tone. "And I hope Amanda's next lesson won't be ruined." I added, just to make sure he felt doubly guilty.

We moved on. Passing the entrance to the hall, Ian noticed something which disagreed profusely with him. There was no door to the hall at this point. There was simply a large open space across which a curtain could be pulled. Frequently, if a teacher was using a video or a CD player, it would be plugged into a socket on a side wall and the wire would be trailed across the entrance. To ensure that nobody tripped over the wire, the teachers would always pull a large mat over it. This system worked well. There had never been an accident caused by someone tripping over the wire. But Ian was not happy.

"You're always having to move the mats, you see." He explained. "Now this is a double problem. Bending over to move the mats could cause a back injury if it's done badly and also, the mats will eventually start to curl up at their edges and become a tripping hazard. You need to find an alternative method. First rule of health and safety, always look at alternative methods."

Above the entrance to the hall was a curtain rail. Ian thought that the solution presented itself admirably through this device. The wires should, he decided, run over the top of the curtain rail, thus keeping the floor totally free from obstruction. He attempted to move the wire straight away but it wasn't long enough to cover its new route. "We'll need an extension cable." He pointed out.

"Oh you will, will you?" Walt remarked. "And that's going to tie up one o' me Jo-Jo reels int it! I'm not made o' bloody Jo-Jo reels, pal." And he disappeared to find the said cable, returning with it a moment later.

"I'll need some step ladders." Ian announced. Walt marched off in the huff to end all huffs and returned with the required step ladders. Before climbing onto them, Ian inspected them thoroughly. Finally, to our astonishment, he gave them a nod of approval and climbed up to perform his task of running the wire over the curtain rail.

With the job complete, he stepped back to admire his handiwork. "You see, it's right out of harm's way now. Nobody can trip over it, nobody needs to move mats around and if you secure the cable to the wall, Walt, they can simply plug in right next to where they're using their machines. In fact, let's do that now." He sent Walt for some cable stays to nail into the wall. Ian positioned the socket bank on the wall at a suitable height. This unfortunately permitted the cable over the entrance to go slack and it drooped in the middle. It did this just as Diane the cook walked through and she stopped, staring at what was now a makeshift noose, hanging from the curtain rail.

"Bloody hell! What yer trying to do, methodise me?" she remarked, to the confusion of all around her. "You could have had me head off. Who are you? Local hangman?" she continued.

"I'm the Health and Safety Officer." Ian announced proudly.

"Chuff me and sprinkle me wi' chopped 'erbs. It gives you faith and that's for sure!" And she walked away, lucky to still be intact after 'dicing' with death, or whatever cooks do when a dangerous situation arises.

Outside, I had something that I wanted to discuss with Ian. I had meant to phone him about it on many occasions but had chickened out because I knew it would force him to come and visit. But now he was here anyway, so it seemed highly appropriate to take him to the place of my concern, the dustbins. School dustbins are a long way removed from the average domestic wheelie bin. They are huge. A small family could live comfortably in a place the size of a school dustbin for many weeks. Over five feet high, six feet long and three feet deep, they were capable of containing almost an entire week's junk mail. But they were on wheels. And ours were positioned at the top of a slope. The slope ended on the school playground and I feared that one day, one of these gargantuan receptacles would break loose and career down the slope and onto the yard. Full of rubbish, its weight would be considerable and once it had gained momentum it would be very hard to stop.

"They're not secure enough." I told Ian. "I'd like to have them in a little compound. Or if that's out of the question, how about some metal posts concreted into the ground to stop them from rolling?"

"You could always do that if you wanted." Ian said. "What do you need to ask me for?"

"Well, it costs. The school budget won't run to another set of biros and I'll never find a few hundred quid for a job like this. Even if I did, I'd need to get it past the governors and they'd claim it wasn't a priority."

"Is it a priority?" Ian asked.

"Well, the moment it becomes one is when you have a bin racing down the hill at forty miles an hour and a group of infants standing on the playground. It's one of those 'hindsight' priorities. I just don't feel comfortable with it."

"I think you're worrying unnecessarily. They have brakes, don't they?"

"They have a bit of metal that pushes against one of the wheels. It's hardly ABS, is it!"

"Well they must have manufacturer's approval. They must have been tested." He stood behind one of the bins and rocked it. "It's a bit flimsy, the brake. But it holds. I can't promise anything, but I'll make a note and look into it for you." He rocked the bin once more, stating that it was fine, and then jotted his note down. Walt and I watched him write and as we did so, we were unaware of the gentle movement of the huge bin by our sides. By the time we noticed it, it had travelled six feet and was picking up speed as it moved downhill.

Walt alerted us to the problem using the descriptive cry of "Shit!" and this prompted us to look round. The bin was accelerating and the three of us began to run after it. As we almost came within touching distance, the path steepened and the bin took on an extra turn of speed. It disappeared from our grasp and we began to run quicker. "We'll never catch this bugger." Walt panted. "Even if we do we can't stop it. It's nearly full. It'll weigh a ton."

That was the point when I realised I could hear children. The morning break time had just begun and the teachers had sent their classes out onto the yard, foolishly thinking they would be safe there. As I spotted the first of the children I shouted, "Get out of the way. Go across the yard."

Walt joined me by shouting, "Bugger off! Shift thisens! Don't stand looking at it, you bloody pancakes!"

One of the supervising teachers came into view at this point. It was Alan Barnett. Seeing an immense dustbin coming his way he blew a whistle to silence the children. "Right, bin approaching rapidly! Other side of yard, pronto. Not going to be pretty – watch it from a distance. Yes." He succinctly announced. The older children understood him and moved away. The younger children followed the older ones but hadn't actually made sense of the instruction.

The final part of the bin's journey entailed dropping down a grass bank onto the yard. It did this with flair. Hitting the bank, it began to spin and it was in this way that it flung itself out of control towards the flatness of the playground. Reaching level ground, it spun twice and rolled over majestically, spilling its contents across the yard. The wind picked up the papers and blew them with abandon as the children began to enjoy this new playtime game of catching flying litter. It was, it must be said, one of the few playtimes in which nobody belted anyone.

As we tried to gather up the rubbish, Ian was approached once again by the little girl he had met in Gillian's room. "Were you looking in there for your rubber?" she asked him. And as he walked away, she surreptitiously placed an old manky rubber into his jacket pocket for him to find at a later moment.

The bin was hard work to push back up the hill. It took a long time and Walt summed it all up perfectly when the job was done by stating, "Well I'm bloody knackered now and I want a piss. Anybody coming?" We declined his kind offer and set off back into the building so that Ian could sign out. Before he did so, we felt the need to investigate a curious noise coming from Ann's office.

Peering round the door I was surprised to see Ann lying on the floor and groaning. "Whatever's happened to you?" I asked. "Is that safety man still here?" was her reply. I confirmed that he was indeed still here. "Well just get him for me, will you?"
Ian appeared in the doorway of Ann's office. She stared at him from her position on the floor and said, "I told you I was happy with my

computer. I told you I didn't mind turning my head slightly to see the screen. Now look what's happened!"

"But how can this be my fault?" Ian asked.

"I was putting a disc thing in the computer thing. It used to be on my desk so I could reach it. But now it's under my desk so I can't. I bent down to find the little hole thing for the disc thing and – well I've got a swivel chair on wheels. The whole thing shot away from under me before I knew what was happening. And now I've gone and hurt my back."

"Forgive me for sounding flippant, but there's only one name for that kind of injury!" I announced.

Ann, clearly not in too much agony, smiled and said, "What's that dear!"

I stood well back in case there were repercussions and announced, "I think it's what's known as a slipped disc."

. "I can't see why they have to have these discos. They play havoc wi' me floors. Tomorrow morning I'll be in here wi' a scrubber. I always end up wi' a scrubber after a disco.

Every lunchtime, two children manned the telephone for half an hour so that Ann could go into the staff room and eat. Children begged to be put on the 'telephone rota' as it was indeed a privilege to be allowed to sit on a swivel chair and take phone messages. And they were very good at it, rarely getting into difficulty.

So it was with a little surprise when Leanne from Year six stopped me on the corridor with a curious message. "Sir, there's a man on the phone and he's looking for a policeman." She said.

"Do you mean he *is* a policeman, Leanne?" I asked her.

"No, he's looking for one." She replied.

"What did you say to him?"

"I said he must have the wrong number because this is a school. But he said that was why he'd rung us and that he needed a policeman urgently."

"Is he still on the line?" I asked her, totally puzzled by this.

"Yes."

"OK, I'll see if I can make any sense of it." I rushed to the office, picked up the phone and began speaking. "Hello, I'm the Headteacher. I believe you need a policeman."

An incredibly strong Indian accent met me from the other end of the line. "Yes I do. I am looking for a pleecment for my daughter. We have moved into the area and I need to get her in school quickly. Do you have a pleecment?"

"Oh, a placement! You want a placement for your daughter at this school! Hold on, let me take some details." Leanne's face flushed with embarrassment as I wrote down the information he gave me. I smiled at her to show that I didn't mind. After all, I think I would have made the same mistake at first.

We were only a week and a half from the end of term and to celebrate the approaching Easter holiday, the Parents' Association had organised a disco for this evening. The Parents' Association was a group of mums and one dad who, every month held an interminable meeting to discuss fund-raising ideas. Basically, they held a couple of discos and a gala each year and much time and energy was put into the planning and preparation of these events. The discos had to be attended by a few staff members for insurance purposes and so some of the teachers were somewhat against too many events taking place. But Gillian and Alan had agreed to join me at tonight's disco as the children ran wild and fell out with each other, to music.

A tradition at the school had been to allow Year Six, the oldest children, to make huge posters to stick up on the hall windows whenever there was a disco. I saw no reason to break with this tradition as it was much enjoyed by the children and took very little time out of the school year. Alan saw things differently, of course and took exception to his class wasting valuable time that could otherwise be spent observing fulcrums.

At two o'clock I visited Year Six to see how their posters were coming along. Alan was sitting glumly at his desk. "Ah, yes, making posters." He told me. "Hate it. Big chunk out of the week, gives the wrong impression about school. I prefer structure, sticking to plans, that sort of thing. You know where you are with plans. I like making plans, it's a thing I do well. Discos, on the other hand, they're not a thing I do well. Not my cup of tea. Don't like tea, actually, prefer hot blackcurrant. Not at a disco though, get it knocked out of your hand. That's the trouble, you see, people everywhere, not aware. And the flashing lights don't help. No, on the whole, not much of a disco lover."

"So, you're looking forward to tonight then?" I asked. "Got a sparkly suit ready? Bit of gel and glitter on the beard? I bet you're unstoppable. That's why all the girls in your class swoon when you go past."

"Ah, never noticed actually. But no, no special outfit, just a nice comfy cardigan."

"And trousers, Alan! You must wear trousers, at least until your beard has grown much, much longer."

"Ah, trousers as well! Goes without saying. Wouldn't make that mistake. Never live it down. I don't like to look a fool. It's not a thing I do well."

"Oh, I don't know!"

I wandered around the room to glean inspiration from the posters. The first child I chanced upon was a rather overweight boy named Jack. He had used a thick, black marker pen to emblazon his poster with the prominent title of 'dico'. I asked him whether he thought he had missed a letter out of the word and his face went red. He ingeniously glued a plain piece of paper over his mistake and once again picked up his marker pen. This time, with bold strokes of his pen, he rewrote his title. When finished, it now proclaimed the word, 'dicso'. I left him to it.

Andrew Dick was the rather unfortunate name of the child sitting nearby. He was a child who had notorious difficulties in making the English language work for him. He could neither spell it, nor speak it very well. Unfortunately, because he could read it with a degree of fluency, the Local Authority would not provide funds to support him with a specialist teacher or assistant. I often wondered whether he had been born a Croatian and would have coped better learning *that* language. His poster was immensely colourful, showing pictures of people dancing and bands playing. It was spoilt because Andrew had chosen to include some words on his otherwise impressive poster. These words invited the onlooker to 'Come and bogie at the praty'. Whether he would be taken up on his offer was open to question. I had my doubts.

Suddenly, Alan made a thrusting announcement from the front of the room. "Right, yes. Well it's, as it were, time for your break. After that you have until two forty-seven to complete your posters. Yes. At that point, we shall, as it were, go and place them on the windows in the hall. We shall then spend the remainder of the afternoon studying seed dispersal. Yes." The children left the room.

When all the children had gone home and the posters were affixed to the windows, it was time to set up a stage area for the DJ. This necessitated assistance from Walt. He arrived in the hall, breathless from an encounter with a urinal. "Right then, let's get this bloody stage job up." were his opening words. I helped him carry the big, wooden blocks across to the chosen spot and we slid them into position. "I can't see why they have to have these discos, I can't." He suddenly commented. "They play havoc wi' me floors, these discos do. I'll tell you this and I'll tell you now, it's because they let 'em eat sweets and have drinks. You get spillage, you see. Tomorrow morning I'll be in here wi' a scrubber. I always end up wi' a scrubber after a disco. And then there's me toilets. I'll tell you this, nah then, I don't even want to talk about me toilets. But all this cleaning I've done tonight, it'll be a waste o' time. They come to these discos specially to make a mess o' me toilets. I'm sure that's why some of 'em come. They don't treat 'em right. You have to respect your toilets, not abuse 'em. I always say, respect your toilet and your toilet'll respect you. Nah then. And I've never been proved wrong. You'll want a piano blocking your egress so they can't get into t'classrooms. Block that corridor off and you're laughing. If they get in a classroom they'll unlock a bloody fire door and then you'll have hell on your hands come locking up time. I don't know why they have these discos, I don't."

Fearing the possibility of entering a conversational loop I made my excuses and found sanctuary in my office. Walt, alternatively, found a loose linkage under a urinal and this gave him something to lavish affection on.

The disco was due to begin at seven thirty and end at nine thirty. To the outside world, this constituted two hours. Inside the hall, with the children satisfying their intake of e-numbers, it would seem like the best part of five years. Children began appearing at six forty-five. Not that I recognised some of them as children at all. Young girls who had been attired in a sensible school outfit just a few hours earlier had returned as sex-crazed vamps. The very same eleven-year-olds who were sitting quietly in assembly this morning had now become seventeen-year-olds with make up and outfits that would make Reverend Bob fall off his Harley Davidson. Young boys who had been so excited at the prospect of Chicken Teddies for lunch were now 'dudes from the hood', dressed in dark t-shirts with offensive slogans printed across their chests. Many, it seemed, needed to hold their left ear in place by pressing a mobile phone against it.

Alan was the first teacher to arrive. Somewhat out of the pupils' league, he was more of a 'dud with a hood'. He wore, as promised, his comfy cardigan. It was grey and had leather patches on the elbows. Perhaps this was to protect the garment if he found himself bursting into an impromptu fit of break dancing, but I would reserve judgement on that. "Lot of children here already." He remarked with hawk-like observation.

"I know. Ruins it, doesn't it!" I replied.

"Already ruined. It's a disco. Can't get worse than a children's disco. I don't enjoy them, never have. Not even as a child. Prefer a good read."

Gillian's car appeared and I prayed that she would not be following the dress code set by the older girls. In the event, she had not changed her outfit since leaving school and this pleased me. Frumpy looked good on Gillian. Anything else would have looked ridiculous, and somewhat intimidating. I knew that the first question

Gillian would ask would be related to the whereabouts of the DJ. It had crossed my mind that the setting up of disco equipment usually takes some time and that time was becoming rather limited. I had tried to put this thought out of my mind on two occasions but it kept returning.

"Hello!" Gillian boomed as I stood to attention. "Is he here yet? The disco man. Has he arrived?"

"No, not yet. I'm getting a bit worried. It's five past seven." I replied.

"Not good enough!" Alan interjected. "Punctuality, that's the key. Like to be punctual. Personal strength of mine, punctuality. Hate to be late. Get flustered, end up with a rash. Lower abdomen, usually, extends down to the genitals, all blotchy. Better to be on time, doesn't happen then. Trouble is, affected by other people's lack of punctuality. Getting a bit worked up now. Feeling the odd itch." Alan put his hand in his pocket and scratched himself. "Hope he hurries up."

"So do I Alan." I announced.

At seven fifteen there was still no sign of the DJ. I announced that I was getting very worried as more and more children were being dropped off by their parents, who would then probably go out for a meal with their phones switched off. Gillian informed me that the secretary of the Parents' Association was the lady setting up the sweet counter, Charlotte Danks. She was the one who should have booked the DJ. I went to speak to her. "Charlotte, can I just check something with you?" I asked.

"Ooh, er, yes. Check something? Ooh, er yes." She replied confidently.

"I just need to know that you definitely booked the DJ for tonight." I explained.

"Booked him, yes. I booked him. I phoned him a few months ago. Yes, I booked him."

"And you definitely gave him today's date?"

"Yes, today's date, yes. That's what it was. It's in my diary, look. Today's date, there it is, disco." She showed me the entry in her diary. It was indeed for today and was sandwiched between 'hair appotment' and 'extra Jim session', about which I dared not ask.

"And did you pay a deposit or anything?"

"Deposit, no. No deposit, he said, till I conformed it in writing."

"And did you?"

"Did I what?"

"Confirm it in writing!"

"Oooh!" She threw her hand over her mouth in realisation of her mistake. She had made a provisional booking but never confirmed it. Consequently, the DJ was not here. I phoned the number on his card and was informed that he was working tonight and was fully booked until three weeks on Monday. This did not help.

I informed Alan and Gillian of the situation and asked if they would go out and try to head off anyone still arriving for the disco. I needed them to turn away anyone who was still with a parent. Alan wondered if he should print out a large notice on the computer and hold it up at the gate. I told him this was an excellent idea but for the fact that all the children would have been dropped off by the time he had produced the thing. He conceded that this was in fact a point he had overlooked and set off up the drive.

Five minutes later he returned, sporting a mournful expression. "Sent back!" he exclaimed.

"Oh dear, been misbehaving?" I asked him.

"No, not that, surplus to requirements. Got it all under control up there, Gillian." He replied.

"Got it all under control everywhere!" I assured him.

"Have to admire her sometimes. Nobody's fool. Knows what she wants. Wish I could be more like that. I'm not assertive, it's not a thing I do well, assertiveness. Too amenable, that's my problem. Too easy going. Can't say that about Gillian, not an easy going sort. Go so far as to say she's hard going. Husband must be a saint. Still, full of admiration for her. Bloody terrifies me though!"

Gillian was doing a sterling job of turning away hoards of children at the gate but the fact remained that we were stuck with at least fifty kids who had turned up for – and wanted – a disco. I hunted desperately through the CD rack in the hope that I might find something suitable to play at a disco. If I could play loud music and flash the lights occasionally, the evening might pass with a small degree of success. But my hopes were dashed as I looked at the school's CD collection. Twelve issues of Great Classics sat at the top of the rack, beneath these were five CDs containing 'All the Hymns You'll Ever Need' and lastly, three sets of 'Everybody's Favourite Nursery Rhymes'. None of these were quite what I had in mind.

Gillian returned and suggested we set up some activities for the children. Alan's suggestion of a good history video that he had in his classroom was turned down flatly. He then pointed out that there was a good programme on the Discovery Channel in twenty minutes about the Greatest Industrial Feats of the Nineteenth Century. He was dismayed to learn that the school had no subscription to this channel as this, in his opinion, would have made the evening pass very quickly indeed.

In the midst of trying to arrest Alan's interest in further wild and wacky schemes, I was aware that Gillian was taking matters into her own hands. She stood on the stage, clapped her hands and miraculously the vamps and the 'dudes' stopped what they were doing and instantly sat, cross-legged on the floor. "Right, you're aware there's no DJ tonight. So I'm afraid you'll have to put up with me taking charge of the proceedings. I hope I didn't just hear somebody groan! We'll begin by playing musical statues. I've been reliably informed that Mr. Barnett can play Frere Jacques with one finger on the piano and so that will suffice as music. Mr. Jeffcock and I will be the judges. Stand up and get into a space."

And so, to Alan's rendition of the well-known French ditty, the Vamps and Dudes indulged in the game with a barely detectable enthusiasm. It was turning out to be just like the wild rave they were hoping for, only entirely different. The thrill of musical statues was followed by more excitement in the form of musical chairs. This was received with a similar level of frenzy as the previous game. After this, it could be reasonably concluded that Alan's musical repertoire was exhausted. This was confirmed by his comment that his finger was becoming sore and this in turn prompted me to ask, out of concern, how his rash was.

After the e-numbers had been consumed the proceedings became a little wild as Alan leapt to the floor and suggested a dancing competition. This was greeted with cheers and Alan clearly was overwhelmed by his new role as saviour of the disco. "Right, yes, it's all set up." he explained. "We'll have ten children out at the front. Five boys and five girls, yes. Now, get on the, er, stage and I'll start the music. Yes. We'll run it for about two minutes and then we'll have, as it were, an election. A vote thing. Everybody can choose the best two boys and the best, as it were, two girls. They can then enter a final round. Does that sound reasonable? Very well." Five cool dudes were chosen from the contingent of boys and they climbed onto the stage and performed curious moves as they limbered up for battle. Five girls dressed in tight tops and mini skirts struggled to lift their lipstick-laden faces onto the stage but once there, they too performed preparatory gyrations. Alan, looking at the array of moves, stood beside them on stage, looking cool in his cardigan. "Goodness. Long time since I could have bent things in that direction. Not good at gyrating, personally. It's not a thing I do well. Far better exercising the remote control finger!" He had made a joke. He chortled uncontrollably for a couple of seconds and then sneezed. "Damn it! Haven't brought a hanky!" he remarked. "Right, are we ready?" To a resounding cry of 'Yes', Alan jumped down from the stage, turned up the volume of the CD player and pressed start.

There was a momentary silence as the CD began to spin. And then the sound of loud music filled the room. Mozart's Fortieth Symphony was booming through the speakers and the cool dancers on stage stood frozen to the spot, with only their eyes moving back and forth. "Come on, let's see some, as it were, cool moves!" Alan shouted, now totally enraptured by the event. The children, not wishing to disappoint, began to perform peculiar movements with their arms and legs. One attempted to carry out a punk-like pogo dance to the symphony whilst others emulated their favourite bands but were clearly having difficulty catching the beat. When the ordeal was over Alan asked the audience to vote for finalists. He did this by asking the children to clap and cheer for each dancer as he pointed to them. The loudest cheers signalled the dubious winners.

"Right, yes, it's the final. Very exciting. Might need the toilet soon. Got to say you all did well. Bet you weren't expecting to dance to Mozart, eh? Nice tune though, often hum it. Got some different music for the final. Test your adaptability. No easy contest, this. If there's one thing I do well, it's organisation and this will be a well organised contest. Yes. Right, into starting positions. One winner only this time. Bag of crisps for the winner, own choice of flavour. Audience, you'll know the song. Join in if you like!" He leapt down and fiddled with the CD player. Within seconds the music was playing. This time the room was filled with the sound of Kum Ba Yah. Alan was singing from the heart and was truly lost in the moment. I would have liked to have been lost in the forest but the opportunity was simply not going to arise. "Join in with the chorus everybody!" Alan shouted, as the dancers frantically looked for ways to strut their stuff to the lyric of 'Someone's Crying Lord'.

It was probably the only time a school disco has passed more slowly for the children than for the adults, but there was little in it as far as I was concerned. As the parents collected their offspring, their conversations warmed my heart. "Have you had a good time?" The parent would ask.

"No, it were crap!" the child would reply. And indeed, their description was devastatingly accurate.

Alan left with renewed enthusiasm for the youth scene. "Should have more evenings like that! I think the children got a lot out of it. Saw a lot of happy faces at the end. Nice event. Rash has gone."

Spring Term: Week 11

"Did Mr. Barnett get us all lost, Miss?" a boy from Alan's class asked.
"I'm afraid so." Celia replied.
"He's a bit of a prat sometimes, isn't he!" the child continued.

It was the very last day before the Easter holiday. Reverend Bob had heard that we were planning an informal Easter Service for the parents to attend and so he invited us to do this in the local church hall. It would make it a community event. It would show that the school and the local church were working in partnership and it would please Reverend Bob's boss – his direct line manager, not his 'ultimate boss', of course.

It would also provide me with a headache. Because of Bob's kind offer, I now had to arrange to walk more than three hundred children half a mile through the pouring rain so that we could sing exactly the same songs and tell exactly the same stories in a draughty church hall instead of in the school hall. However, in the name of community liaison, it had all been agreed two weeks previously and the parents had been duly invited to St. Mark's Church Hall.

The service was to begin at two o'clock. At one o'clock, we ensured that every child in the school had visited the toilet, whether or not they had any wish to do so. The children would be walked to the church hall class by class, starting with the oldest because they both walked faster and could cope better with waiting for everyone else at the other end of the journey. Alan was therefore to start the process at one fifteen. He assured me he knew a good short cut to the hall and he promised to send the last child from his class to tell Celia to set off with her class. And so the system would continue, with each class letting the next youngest class know when they had left. An immense snake of children soon began to weave its way down the drive and along the road, disappearing into a little hidden pathway which formed the beginning of the short cut.

With the last class out of the building I left Ann and Walt in charge and set off to join the back of the snake. It was one thirty-five. The narrow pathways formed an incomprehensible maze through the estate. From time to time we would emerge into the apparent civilisation of a real road, only to plunge into another concealed path a moment later. Eventually, after many disorientating turns, I rounded a corner to find the entire school standing outside a building and waiting, I presumed, for someone to let them in. I bypassed the children and walked to the front of the line where Alan was stroking his beard frantically. This signalled trouble to me.

The sign above the door proudly informed us that we had arrived at Hilltop Community Centre. I hoped with all my heart that this was a secret code name for St. Mark's Church Hall, but I had a sickening feeling that it wasn't. Alan came across to me, still stroking his beard.

"Usually good with directions." He proclaimed. "Not this time though. Don't understand it, finding my way around is normally a thing I do well. Sure the place is supposed to be here. Couldn't have moved it, could they? Wouldn't be the first time I've turned up somewhere and found they've moved it."

"Have you got any idea where we are, Alan?" I asked him.

"Not a clue!" he replied.

It didn't look good. Getting lost on one's own was perhaps excusable. But getting lost with an entire school in tow was verging on the humiliating. Celia came over to ask what was going on.

"Got us lost, I'm afraid." Alan admitted. "Normally good with directions. Curious little pathways that shot it for me. Didn't come out where I hoped they would. Won't use them again. Learning from mistakes is a thing I do well."

"We're five roads away." Celia said. "I know where we are because I've driven poorly kids home around here. You get with my class, Alan, and I'll go up front."

A child from Alan's class tapped Celia on the arm. "Did Mr. Barnett get us all lost, Miss?" he asked.

"I'm afraid so." Celia replied.

"He's a bit of a prat sometimes, isn't he!" the child continued.

Celia smiled.

At one fifty-eight, we entered the church hall. Reverend Bob was looking a little flustered but was nevertheless relieved to see us. The hall was almost full of parents and squeezing the children in was a fearsome job. I asked people to open windows so that we would all be in with a chance of breathing and I gave thanks that Walt hadn't joined us. As the children were sitting down, Bob pulled me to one side.

"I want to show you my organ!" he announced. Feeling that doing this in such a public place might result in a rapid defrocking, I was hesitant at first. But he pointed to a musical instrument at the front of the hall and my panic subsided. "Got it for Iris. She's the organist down here. She's eighty-four but she's brilliant on the keys." He explained to me that until this week, Iris had been forced to play an old harmonium, transferred from the previous church hall thirty years ago. Playing such a beast necessitated the constant pumping of two pedals which blew air into the instrument. The air was what produced the sound. Fearing that Iris was one day likely to expire if she was required to pump and play well into her dotage, Reverend Bob had raised money for a rather impressive electronic organ. Thus, Iris could perform her duties without feeling she had run a half marathon by the end of the service. And today, Bob informed me, would be her first time on his organ!

Things began well, if a little late. Bob introduced the service and welcomed everyone to the church hall. He announced the first hymn and everyone tried to stand. This was difficult as the space was limited but ultimately, everyone was on either their own, or someone else's feet. Iris, as promised, was an excellent organist. She played the introduction to the first hymn perfectly, if a little loud. But then, as the children began to sing, the organ fell silent. Seconds later it boomed out at an ear-shattering volume and then dropped once more to virtual silence. The waves of piercing volume and sudden silence continued for the whole of the first verse and as I looked across at Iris, I could see her frantically pumping the swell pedal on her electronic organ. The swell pedal, of course, is a volume control – press it down for loud and let it up for soft. Iris was confusing this with the bellows of her harmonium, believing that she needed to pump air into the system to make the instrument play.

Bob whispered in her ear and she tried, not completely successfully, to leave the swell pedal alone for the rest of the hymn. Save for the occasional startling change of volume, things progressed more agreeably from that point. At the end of the hymn, everyone attempted to sit down. The children were sitting on the floor and manoeuvring themselves into position in such crowded circumstances took almost as long as the hymn had taken. But finally, with everybody seated, Bob stood up to speak. "Our first reading will be read by Sophie Smith from Year Five. Would you like to come out, Sophie?" Sophie would have loved to come out. Unfortunately, from her position in the middle of the group, this act took some considerable time and involved her treading on seven children's fingers and two children's legs as she fruitlessly attempted to find areas of floor on which she could walk. At last, with nine children writhing in agony, Sophie made it to the lectern.

She spoke beautifully. Her voice rang clear throughout the hall and I felt very proud of her. I could see her mother, almost preening herself as her daughter impressed everyone in the building. Sophie's confidence increased and she began to relax in front of her audience. And then, without warning, a deafening blast of noise issued forth from Iris the organist. A cacophony of notes from the organ rioted through the church hall and visibly terrified Sophie, who seemed to believe that the hand of God was approaching to give her a good slapping.

Iris was in fact preparing for the next hymn. In the past, she had placed her music book on the keys of her harmonium. If she was not pumping air into the instrument, it would not play and so she disturbed nobody. The electronic organ was different. It remained permanently ready for action whilst it was switched on. And Iris had placed her book atop eight keys so that she could find the next page. And every one of those eight keys had blasted out its note with a sound as far removed from harmony as it seemed possible to attain.

The second hymn remained at much more of a constant volume than had the first, with only the occasional pumping of the pedal during a moment of concentration lapse. The major event, for me at least, during the hymn was the arrival of the Mad Woman. Clearly put out by being late, she closed the door behind her with a bang and pushed her way through the crowd of parents standing at the back of the room. Reaching the area where chairs were set out she looked somewhat annoyed that no seat had been reserved for her and stood, sighing loudly, at the edge of the room whilst closely watching 'Our Michael' to ensure the vicar was not bullying him.

The service ended at two fifty. Everyone agreed that it had been a pleasant way to spend the last afternoon of term and that the children, and ultimately Iris, had done very well. It was now time to return the children to school and by general consensus, Celia was going to lead the way. But my afternoon was degenerating rapidly because I could see the Mad Woman approaching and my thoughts were not appropriate for my ecclesiastical surroundings.

"I've been to school to see this service!" she snapped. "Nobody told me you were bringing everybody down here. I got to school and they said you'd all gone to St. Mark's Hall."

"We sent a letter out nearly two weeks ago." I assured her.

"Not to me, you didn't!" she argued. "It's always the same. You tell everybody else but not me. It makes me look a fool and you do it on purpose!"

"We don't send out selective letters. If you didn't get one, all I can suggest is that it must still be in Michael's bag."

"They used to put it with his reading book when he were younger. They don't do that now. It's to make sure I don't get me letters!"

"No, he's older. We don't spoon-feed older children like we do with infants. We expect them to take a bit of responsibility. It's the same for every child once they're in the juniors."

She snorted and walked away. I took the opportunity and walked the other way, ushering the children out of the door and into the rain. The journey back to school was strangely shorter than the journey to the church hall. Many parents walked back with us and we allowed the children to collect their belongings and set off five minutes early if their parents were waiting.

We had a rule regarding absent parents at 'home time'. If a child expected to be picked up by someone and that 'someone' wasn't waiting outside, the child had to come inside and tell us. We would then make a phone call and look after the child until someone arrived. In the past, one parent – unbeknown to us – had offered to take a distressed child home with her when its mother hadn't arrived. Whilst this had seemed helpful on the surface, it was the worst thing she could have done. When the distressed child's mother appeared fifteen minutes late, she came into school to collect her daughter only to find that we had neither got her, nor knew where she was. She was understandably upset – and less understandably abusive – thinking her daughter had been abducted. From that moment our policy was made crystal clear to every parent and the new system worked well.

Tonight's 'left-over child' was Our Michael. This was highly unusual as his mother was normally waiting on the yard from around eleven thirty in the morning. It was even more unusual as I had just left her at the church hall. I sat Our Michael down and went to phone his house. Mr. Mad Woman answered and seemed confused that nobody was there to pick him up.

"She came to the church." I said. "Was she likely to go anywhere after that?"

"Not that I know of." Replied the man, who sounded very ordinary and sensible.

"Perhaps she's stopped to chat to somebody." I suggested.

"I wouldn't have thought so. Nobody talks to her, she's a nutter!" he replied, proving my earlier assessment of his personality.

"Well, let's hang on a bit. I'll ring you if there's no sign of her later." I reassured him.

I hung up and prepared to tell Our Michael that I couldn't trace her. I thought he might want to have a party to celebrate. But before I reached him the phone rang again and I went back to answer it. On the other end of the line was the Mad Woman.

"I can't talk long, I'm on my mobile and it's too expensive!" she announced. "Is our Michael there?"

"Yes, he's waiting in the entrance hall. Will you be long?" I asked.

"Well I don't know, do I! All I know is that they've gone too far this time. I'll be complaining very high up, I will." She yelled.

"I'm sorry, I don't understand. Where are you and what's gone wrong?"

"I'm where you last saw me, that's where I am. I'm in the church hall and it's not funny. I'm locked in." I had to disagree – it was funny. It was very funny, but I did my best to sound serious and concerned.

"You're locked in? Didn't you leave with everyone else?" I asked with tears rolling down my face.

"No I flipping didn't! I suffer with me bowels, I do. I've seen a doctor but he's useless. I've complained to t'Medical Council about him and they're looking into it. I want him struck off! Anyway, I've got this bowel problem and when I have to go I have to go. So I went." She fell silent for a moment.

"Carry on." I suggested. This was the first time I actually wanted to listen to what she had to say.

"Well sometimes it takes me a while once I get in there. I didn't know they were going to lock up and go home, did I! I came out of t'ladies and t'place were deserted. Every door's locked and t'windows only open at t'top. Little slits, they are, high up. So I'm stuck and it's lucky I had t'school phone number in me mobile."

"I'll ring the vicar. I'll get him to go back down and let you out and I'll keep Michael here until you arrive." I told her. "Don't go anywhere, will you!"

In a fit of laughter I rang Reverend Bob and then proceeded to inform every member of staff about the Mad Woman's plight. It was a perfect end to a term and many people had huge smiles on their faces as they walked around the building.

"Bugger me backwards! Somebody come and look at this!" Came a shout that could only be attributed to Walt. It was now fifteen minutes since I had phoned Reverend Bob and as the Mad Woman had not yet arrived, I decided to go and look at the object of Walt's enthusiasm. He was looking out of Ann's window and had already been joined by Amanda, Paul and Alma, all of whom were laughing uncontrollably. I arrived in the room to see the reason for the merriment. Reverend Bob had returned the Mad Woman. She was sitting astride his Harley Davidson, wearing her powder blue anorak and with her skirt pulled up beyond her knees, exposing her short, sock-length tights and varicose veins. The deeply tinted helmet provided a welcome improvement over her what was usually seen above her neck. She staggered off the bike, hopping sideways for quite some distance, before coming to rest against the bonnet of Paul's car. This act triggered the alarm and as it sounded, she leapt away from the vehicle in panic and then proceeded to spend the next three minutes attempting to break free from the grip of the helmet. "You wouldn't want to find one o' them round yer U bend, and I'll tell you that. Nah then!" Walt suggested. "Well my cream egg's going to have to wait till tomorrow now! I shan't be wanting to eat wi' a picture of that in me head!"

She picked up Michael, told him off about something and they marched briskly way. Walt mentioned something about her being the one thing that could scare the shit out of a Hell's Angel and then explained that he would like to lock up early. He was off to his caravan at the seaside tonight so he wanted us to bugger off home.

We all obliged. It was holiday time.

Final Words

Two terms in and I was now feeling really confident – really confident that I hadn't a clue what to expect from one minute to another. Still, we had passed our inspection and still had a little room to go downhill before the next one.

There was one term remaining before my first year was complete. During next term, although I didn't know it yet, we would have a bomb scare, I would find parents snogging on the school trip and Alan would spend time walking around with a large stapler dangling from his trousers. All in all, pretty much what I had come to expect.

'More Repressed Memories of a Primary School Headteacher' is the third and final book of the series and documents just how crazy things become as the school year draws to a close.

Thanks for reading.

Books by Peter Jeffcock – all available right now on Kindle

For updates, quotes and other information, follow me on Twitter @peterAjeffcock and find me on Facebook at Peter Jeffcock Books.

A PIS OF CAK (Humour)

The original, best selling Pis of Cak is now available on Kindle. Bursting with unintentional humour, written by children when they are trying to be serious, this book has amused and delighted thousands of readers for over 10 years. Revel in the imagery of 'wild breasts roaming the jungle', update your knowledge of history by learning that there was a law 'demanding sexy quality for women', or simply smile at the idea that 'suspension bridges hang from a cloud'. Enter a world where haemorroids fly through space and where children in wartime had to be evaporated for their own safety and you may never view life in quite the same way again.

The A Pis of Cak series is now up to four books…

ANOTHER PIS OF CAK (Humour)
A THIRD PIS OF CAK (Humour)

A PIS OF CAK – THE FOURTH SLICE (Humour)

THE HEADTEACHER DIARIES: (Humour)

- **Headlong Into Chaos – The Diaries of a Primary School Headteacher**
- **Get Me Out Of Here – I'm A Headteacher**
- **More Repressed Memories of a Primary School Headteacher**

This series of three books document the author's first year as Head of a School in a North Midlands former mining town in the 1990s. It is hard to imagine what goes on behind the scenes of an apparently normal primary school and as the new Head starts out in his new post he meets his techno-phobic secretary, his terrifying deputy head and his incredibly foul-mouthed caretaker who has an obsession with polishing his urinals and categorising his nuts. With an array of parents that range from delightful to the insane (where insane makes up a huge majority) and a staff of rather eccentric teachers, life is never going to be easy. Every day brings about a new set of unexpected and bizarre problems that somehow interfere ever so slightly with the normal running of the school. From 50 children vomiting in unison during an assembly to getting the whole school locked outside during a fire drill, every day, indeed every minute, has the makings of a peculiar sitcom.

BEYOND THE FRAME (Sci-Fi Adventure)

Ross Carter has a unique ability. He can slip into old photographs and interact with the people in the pictures. After his boss asks for help in saving his wayward brother from an untimely death back in the 1960s, Carter accepts the mission. He travels back and prevents the young man from being killed, but when Carter returns to the present time he finds the brother's influence has changed everything for the worse. Carter has no job, no wife, no home and the man who was his boss is now dead – killed by the brother Carter had saved. His only chance of putting everything right is to go back and ensure that the brother dies, as he originally did. But once he returns to the past he meets up with an adversary who is hell bent on saving the brother's life – he meets himself...

MAD MAN – 100 Airport Codes to Brighten your Boarding Pass (Humour)

When the author noticed that a flight from Madrid to Manchester appeared on his ticket as MAD MAN, it prompted him to find out what other great journeys might be lurking out there. It turns out there are quite a few. If you want to know how to find HOT SEX, TOY BOY, FAT BUM or even DOC TOR WHO on your airline ticket, this is the book that tells you which flight to check on to.

PINK KNICKERS AND STUN GUNS (Comedy Adventure)

Even the kindest of people would describe Jemma Spicer as a complete flake! And when she inadvertently picks up the wrong bag from the airport carousel she sparks a series of events that place her in mortal danger. The bag's owner is desperate to get his luggage back before anyone discovers its extraordinary contents. But Jemma has already found them. And what she has discovered catapults her into the middle of an evil crime ring, threatening millions of lives – especially hers.

With only her delightfully scatty logic and the items in the bag to help her, she must stop one of the world's most powerful techno-criminals from destroying the future of her country. But first she has to work out what he is up to. How can an ordinary girl save an entire nation? How will she ever get over the trauma of a life and death pedalo chase! And should she really do that to the Queen?

If James Bond had been a fashion-obsessed girl who seemed to have absolutely no idea of what was going on around him, he would have been indistinguishable from Jemma herself.

THE ECONOMY DRIVE (Money Saving)

Use this book as if it is a distance learning project. Learn how to drive in a fantastically fuel-efficient way, whilst not sacrificing any of the fun of driving. You don't have to drive like a snail to be economical – and this book gives you all the methods. You will save serious money each year on fuel if you follow these simple methods.

JASON MASON'S SECOND WIND (Teenage Humour)

Sports day is approaching at Upper Gumtree School and Jason Mason is dreading it. He is the slowest runner in the class and, when under pressure, his legs seem to develop a mind of their own, causing him to stagger and wobble in a variety of directions as he attempts to keep up with his classmates. And if this were not bad enough, the class bully, Sam Lamb is, according to Jason, possibly the fastest runner in the entire world. But when Jason buys a particular brand of lemonade, he discovers it has an effect on him that is truly mind blowing – except the blowing doesn't come from his mind! And suddenly sports day feels far less scary.

Printed in Great Britain
by Amazon